Racing Toward Providence

Laurel Mills

RACING TOWARD PROVIDENCE
© 2008 BY LAUREL MILLS

ISBN 10: 1-933113-92-8
ISBN 13: 978-1-933113-92-0

First Printing: 2008

This Trade Paperback Is Published By
Intaglio Publications
Walker, LA USA
WWW.INTAGLIOPUB.COM

CREDITS
EXECUTIVE EDITOR: TARA YOUNG
Cover design by Valerie Hayken, www.valeriehayken.com.
and Sheri graphicartist2020@hotmail.com.

ACKNOWLEDGMENTS

I wish to thank the Ragdale Foundation for providing a quiet and nurturing environment in which to write. I am also grateful to the University of Wisconsin-Fox Valley for grants that allowed time to work on this manuscript.

Thank you to my writing group for inspiration, advice, and encouragement: Ellen Kort, Marge Higgins, and Rusty McKenzie. My gratitude also for the feedback of readers Jackie Calhoun, Joan Hendry, Nina Rowland, Lori Peterson, and Marie Sawall. I am especially grateful to Alice Danahy for giving me a tour of the city of Providence.

I appreciate the hard work and dedication of Sheri Payton, Kate Sweeney, and Tara Young of Intaglio Publications. You are all a joy to work with!

My loving gratitude to my family who shared many experiences with me in Maine: Maureen and Butch Riggs, Brad and Mary Lothrop, and Sherryl Porter. And thank you to Josh for inspiring the story with his resilient spirit.

As always, I am most grateful to Lynn, steadfast and sure in her love and support.

For Lynn Abitz Koss, as always.

We are all one child spinning through Mother Sky.
— Shawnee proverb

Chapter 1

Jean McCray and I probably had the shortest love affair on record. Thirteen days. Looking back on it now, I don't know why it took nearly two weeks for us to realize we were better off as friends than as lovers. As lovers, we were dismally mismatched. As friends, we got along fine most of the time.

Our short love affair, which took place during our sophomore year at the Rhode Island School of Design, was clumsy and awkward. We even looked funny together. Jean had a stocky build; she was taller than me and at least fifty pounds heavier. I admired the aura of strength and sturdiness that emanated from her, but I wasn't really attracted to her physically. As I said, it didn't take long for us to get back to being just friends.

Jean was the one who convinced me years later to move to Maine from Providence. I was ready for a change, tired of working as a gallery curator and not having enough time to work on my own art. When she offered to sell me a mountain cabin close to hers in the western part of the state, I envisioned an idyllic existence where I'd be free to paint from morning to night if I wanted.

When I told my family I was moving, my mother and my brother, Dan, warned me that I would be lonely on the mountain and would miss Providence, and I have to admit I did miss the cultural aspects that city life offers. I missed the art galleries, the theater, the Italian restaurants on Federal Hill, shops and cafés on Thayer Street, good bookstores, and clubs where I would go to listen to live music. And I missed seeing my family, especially my nephew Timmy, who liked me to take him out for ice cream whenever I could fit him into my schedule.

But here I was, living in happy solitude in Maine. The life

I'd created for myself on Hurricane Mountain was entirely of my own making, and I'd go to most any lengths to keep it just the way it was.

My habit was to begin my day painting in my studio just after daybreak when the light was good. The ceiling-to-floor windows on each end of the loft, along with skylights in the steeply pitched roof, bathed the studio in light. My studio was a jumble of paints and canvases, but I loved it. I could leave things where I wanted, undisturbed by anyone but me.

One early June day, I worked into mid-afternoon, then put away my brush and went outside to trim weeds near the front step. It was a scorching day with a flawlessly blue sky. Because I was sweltering in the heat and feeling a wonderful sense of freedom this far from civilization, on impulse I stripped off my shirt, down to my sports bra. The sun on my exposed back felt glorious, its warmth massaging my tired shoulders after a morning spent standing at an easel. I never expected a strange man's voice to break the silence.

"That's a waste of time. It'll just grow back."

I dropped my clipping shears and nearly jumped out of my skin. People didn't just show up on this isolated mountain. As the masculine voice resonated in my ears, I felt exposed. Instinctively, I threw one arm over my breasts and scrabbled around in the grass with my other hand for my T-shirt. I pulled it hurriedly over my head. It was inside out and stuck with bits of grass that made my skin itch.

"Didn't mean to scare you," the deep voice behind me said.

Shoving the tail of my shirt into the waist of my shorts, I jumped to my feet and swung around to face him. He stood just a few feet away in an army green shirt, camouflage pants, and combat boots. Under a fatigue cap, his graying hair hung in strands over his ears and neck, brushing against his collar.

"Who are you?" I demanded, fists on my hips.

Looking down at me, the stranger said, "No need to get upset." He was of husky build and easily outweighed my 123 pounds. I wondered if I should be afraid, if he meant harm.

I pulled myself to my full height of 5'5", but I was still aware that he towered over me. "This is private land."

"Didn't mean to upset you," he said. "I was hiking on the other side of the mountain, following a deer path, and this is where I ended up." He pulled an apple from a canvas fanny pack and tossed it from one hand to another like a baseball. Then he unsnapped a leather case on his belt and lifted out a knife, sun glinting off the steel blade. Keeping his eyes on me, he sliced a piece from the blood red apple. He speared the white flesh with the tip of the knife and carried it to his mouth, bringing the blade dangerously close to his lips. As he bit into the apple, a morsel fell onto his shirtfront.

I was becoming more and more nervous, but did my best to hide it. "What's your name?"

He smiled, and I noticed that a front tooth was chipped. "What a nice spot this is," he said, slicing off another piece of apple. "One of the prettiest places in this part of Maine, I bet."

I felt the muscles in my face tighten. This man's uninvited presence on my land infuriated me. "Your name?" I insisted.

"I won't tell you what my friends call me." He chuckled as he looked down at me. "Most folks use Garret." Again he lifted the knife blade, carrying a slice of apple to his mouth.

"Well, Garret, what are you doing on Hurricane Mountain?"

He swiped his mouth with the back of his hand and chucked the remaining portion of apple over his shoulder. It seemed he wasn't going to answer my question, so I asked again, "Just why are you here?" I was becoming impatient with him.

"Nice day, don't you think?" he said. "But damn hot." He wiped the knife blade on his pants and slipped it back into its sheath. It was a relief to see him put the knife away and snap the leather case. "I'm interested in buying a piece of land around here," he said casually, as if he were commenting on the weather again. "It looks like good hunting. I could pull a little trailer up here somewhere and hunt right out my backyard."

My stomach knotted at his words. "There isn't any land for sale anywhere near here."

"Oh, yeah?" He looked around, his eyes gauging what he

3

saw: meadows full of blueberry bushes; woods lush with not only evergreens, but also maple, oak, birch, and beech trees; humpback mountains all around; a near-perfect blue sky overhead. "Not many people around, are there? Looks like plenty of unsettled space."

I was aware that we were the only two humans within hollering distance. Jean was at The Village Store she owned in Clayton, and our neighbor Bernice Slade was seldom around on weekdays. She was a widow, and during the week, she usually stayed at the house she'd owned with her husband in Fredericksville, where she worked in the paper mill.

"The paper mill owns most of the land on this mountain," I said. "They do some logging." I was impatient to get rid of this trespasser, and I heard the hard edge to my voice. "What's left belongs to private owners like me."

He pulled a plastic water bottle from the canvas pack at his waist and flipped the top with his thumb. "Maybe you'd be kind enough to let me hunt on your land. Seems like you're in a prime position here on the mountain." His words made me cringe at the thought of him—or anyone else—carrying a rifle onto my land and intruding on my safe haven.

"That wouldn't be possible." While I was talking, I noticed that he continued to take in my cabin and spread of land.

"How many acres do you own?" He tossed the question out, then leaned his head back and squirted water into his mouth.

"Look, I think you'd better be going."

"Hey, take it easy. I'm just passing through." He strapped the water bottle back into the canvas pack. "If you ever change your mind about selling your land, let me know. I'm the only Garret Belling in the Fredericksville phone book." When he smiled, I couldn't decide if his grin was friendly or sinister.

"I won't be changing my mind." Sell? Not after I'd worked all of my thirty-four years to get to this place, to have the freedom to live as I desired: a happy recluse. I wanted him off my property now. "You got a vehicle around here?"

"I walked in, and I'll walk out," he said, but he didn't make any move to leave. He lifted off his cap and pushed strands of hair behind his ears. After slapping the cap against his thigh, he replaced it on his head.

"You can follow my driveway out to the gravel road." I pointed in the opposite direction from which he'd come. "And the next time you want to go hiking on the mountain, remember that this is private property." We were interrupted by the sound of a vehicle whining its way up the road. As a red pickup pulled into my yard, I was relieved to realize it was Jean. She must have come home from the store for a lunch break. I waved with both hands high in the air. I couldn't remember ever being so glad to see anyone as I was to see her right then.

She jumped down from the driver's seat. "Got company?" she asked as she walked toward us.

"He's just leaving," I said.

"Good afternoon, ladies," the stranger said, touching the brim of his cap and nodding at us. He headed with long strides toward the sandy driveway, patting the front fender of Jean's truck as he walked past. Her German shepherd, Badger, was lying in the truck bed and jumped to his feet, growling. The man stopped and talked to the dog in a deliberately soft voice. "Hey, feller, can't someone around here make a guy feel welcome?" He turned and waved to us, tipping his cap, before he headed down the lane.

Jean and I watched until he disappeared. "What was that all about, Samantha?"

"I don't really know. He just turned up here. His name's Garret Belling. Said he's looking for hunting land."

Jean batted at a deerfly that was buzzing near her face. "Well, he can just keep on looking—elsewhere."

"That's what I told him."

"Hey, I've got to get going." Jean opened the truck door and hoisted herself up onto the seat. "I just came home for a short break, then Badger and I head back to the store."

"Watch for Garret on the way out."

She stuck her head out the truck window. "Run him down, you mean?"

I grinned as she drove off in the direction of her log cabin. I pictured her chasing Garret Belling down the mountain with her truck. If anyone could do it, it was Jean McCray.

Good. I hope she scares him off. Having a stranger walk onto my property had made me nervous. I resented the interruption to my peaceful existence. "Damn him." I swore under my breath as I picked up the clippers I'd dropped. "Well, just damn it," I said again when I pricked my finger on the sharp point. As I sucked the blood from the tip of my finger, I hoped it wasn't a sign of things to come.

The next morning, I drove down the mountain to Clayton, a tiny village that swelled with vacationers in the summer. Drawing most of the tourists was Lake Rand, a large lake ringed by low-lying mountains. Right at the center of the crossroads stood The Village Store where you could get groceries, gas, beer, and lots of free advice from Jean McCray. As I passed through the village, I noticed Jean sitting on the wide front step of her store, talking to a tourist. I tooted my horn at her, and she waved before she leaned back into her conversation. I continued along thirteen miles of winding, paved road that led to the larger town of Fredericksville, where I stopped at the hardware store and bought a stack of *No Trespassing* signs. I was not going to be surprised again by strangers sneaking up behind me on my own land.

All afternoon, I trudged in the hot sun, posting the perimeter of my eighty acres on Hurricane Mountain. I walked through meadows of tall grass and wild daisies, through forests thick with underbrush, up and down steep slopes. Sweat was running down my face, and I had to keep wiping my brow with my forearm. The Cutters I'd coated myself with kept the mosquitoes and tiny black flies from biting, but they hummed and droned in a cloud around my head. As I pounded a nail into a pine tree, I reminded myself, *I came to this mountain to get away from interruptions and distractions.* Selfish? Perhaps, but that was the reason I chose to live here.

After I nailed the last notice onto a weathered fencepost, I stepped back and admired the black and orange sign: *No Trespassing/No Hunting.* Satisfied, I headed back to my cabin, swinging the hammer by the handle as I walked.

I felt safer now that I'd posted my property. Maybe that would keep stray wanderers off my land. Curled up on the futon couch in front of the stone fireplace, I sipped a glass of mango juice as I read the weekly letter from my mother. She caught me up on the goings-on in Providence and filled me in on news about my family. My brother and I didn't correspond very often. At Christmas and on my birthday, I'd get a card, but I knew his wife, Jennifer, had picked it out and signed it. Any news I got of Dan was through my mother, although mostly her letters were full of reports about Timmy:

Can you believe Timmy will be in third grade next fall? He's growing up so fast! Of course, right now he's enjoying summer vacation. I watch him a few days each week, and he goes to day camp the other days. Dan says it's a good recreational program— the kids play games and do arts and crafts. His best friend Darnell goes to the day camp, too, and Timmy is always full of stories of the activities they do there.

A piece of lined notebook paper was also in the envelope. I pulled it out and unfolded it to discover a picture that Timmy had drawn for me. I taped the crayon drawing of a rocket blasting off, on the door of my refrigerator. Stepping back to admire it, I realized the perspective wasn't right, but the flames he'd colored at the bottom of the rocket were quite realistic. Maybe he'd inherited his Aunt Sam's knack for art.

I was still sitting on the futon reading a book when Jean drove past my cabin to her house. In the dark, I could hear her truck door open and close and Badger barking. I hit the sack right after that, and my last thought before I fell asleep was that I hadn't told Jean about posting the *No Trespassing/No Hunting* signs. Evidently, she hadn't noticed them on the way home in the dark or I would have heard about it.

The next morning on her way to the store in the daylight, the posters must have grabbed Jean's attention. At 6:30 a.m., she called me. I was still asleep, and the ringing of the phone startled me into semi-consciousness. I fumbled for it on the pine headboard that served as bookcase and catchall, knocking over a box of tissues, then the silent alarm clock. Finally, my hand found the familiar shape. "Hello," I groaned, my eyes still closed.

"What the hell are you trying to do, Samantha Warren? Ruin my business?"

"Jean, what's the matter?" I mumbled.

"Get your ass down here to the store pronto. I want to talk with you. But first, tear down those damn signs." In the background, I could hear the bell jingle over the store door. Jean lowered her voice. "You'll have every sportsman from here to Massachusetts pissed at us. I can't afford that." She slammed the receiver down, and I was left with the phone line buzzing in my ear.

I didn't drive down the mountain to the store right away. I didn't take down the posters, either. In fact, I took the phone off the hook. *Let Jean fume if she wants to. I'm going to leave the signs right where they are.* Jean no longer owned this piece of land. She'd sold it to me, and I would decide how it was going to be used. If she wanted strangers on her property, so be it. I didn't.

After Jean's phone call, I carried a cup of steaming tea upstairs to the loft studio and cleared a spot for it on the worktable. I put together several frames, mitering the corners of slats, then pounded brads in to hold them together. My tea grew cold while I worked, stapling canvas over the edges of the frame, then applying gesso, which would tighten the canvas as it dried. The gesso would also act as a primer, allowing paint to adhere to the canvas. At noon, I quit and carried the cup of cold tea downstairs.

By the time I arrived at The Village Store, Jean hadn't cooled down much since her phone call. Even before I was fully inside the door, she started harping at me. "About time you got here, Samantha Warren!" Jean always called me by my full name when she was angry with me. "I can't believe you actually posted *No Hunting* signs. What were you thinking anyway?" She whispered so the customers wouldn't hear her, but her voice was sharp. "Did you take them down like I told you?"

"Not yet."

An angry blush reddened her cheeks. "Not yet? What the hell

are you waiting for?"

I tried to explain. "I don't see what harm a few *No Trespassing* signs can make. It's less than eighty acres, for heaven's sake, out of that whole mountain."

"Yeah. But it's right in the middle of prime hunting territory. And nobody can get to my 106 acres without going through your property, so essentially you've posted my land, too." She pulled a tray of mushrooms out of the refrigerator and set it on the deli counter.

"Honestly, Jean, I hadn't thought of that."

"Did you stop to think that hunters won't be able to get through to the old Bailey farm, either? Your land blocks that trail, too. The old apple orchard up there has a number of hunting stands in it, and just how are people going to get to them?" Her voice rose, and her hand moved rapidly, slicing the mushrooms.

I put a finger to my lips to remind Jean to keep her voice down. "I still don't see what's the big deal. There are plenty of places to hunt on Hurricane Mountain. I just don't want anyone hunting on my land."

She scooped the chopped mushrooms into a stainless steel bowl. "The thing is," she said, looking at me as if I were a child, "once it gets out that the land next to me, the land I used to own, is posted, I won't have just a drop in business. I'll have *no* business. Everyone will go to The Other Store across the street. Or they'll go to Fredericksville to do their shopping. You tell the locals they can't hunt, and they'll go miles out of their way if they have to just to boycott me."

"You'll still have plenty of tourist business."

"Just during the summer months. You know damn well I depend on the locals, especially sportsmen, to keep the store going the rest of the year." Jean dropped her voice as a customer came to the counter with a bag of charcoal briquettes and a can of starter fluid. She wiped her hands on her apron and began to ring up the purchase.

As I was leaving the store, Jean called to me, "Do it today, Sam." Clearly, she thought she'd won the argument.

But I wasn't ready to give in. I was determined to leave the signs right where I'd posted them.

Still rattled by Jean's reaction, I drove the gravel road that scaled Hurricane Mountain. As I got closer to my cabin, I couldn't believe what I saw: Somebody had ripped down the signs I'd posted. Where my property line ran along the gravel road, orange and black fragments clung to nail stubs on trees and fence posts.

I slammed the flat of my hand on the steering wheel. "Damn that Bernice," I swore out loud. It would be just like her to tear down the signs. A tough old bird, even in her sixties, she was a force to be dealt with. We'd never gotten along; from the moment I'd moved here, we were at odds. She looked like an aging Vegas chorus girl, always dressed in knit pants and plunging knit tops that hugged her body and revealed more than anyone would want to see. Dangling earrings made her earlobes sag, and cheap bracelets clattered at her wrist. Her nails were painted red, and her eyes were smudged with dark eyeliner and green eye shadow. But she was a dynamo, independent as all get out. She'd been alone since her husband died a few years earlier of cirrhosis. I thought maybe Bernice was headed down that path, too, because she often seemed drunk when she was at her cabin.

I was ready to pull into my neighbor's yard and ask if she was responsible for destroying my signs, but as I approached her cabin, there was no indication that she was around.

Across the road from Bernice Slade's cabin, I drove down the lane toward my A-frame. Along this edge of my property, too, only scraps hung on the trees, as if the posters had been ripped off hastily. I pulled into the dirt drive in front of my cabin and sat with my hands on the wheel, fuming. Who had done this? Who'd had the audacity to come onto my property and remove my signs?

I shut off the motor, jumped down from the Jeep, and stomped to my front door. As I reached for the latch, I noticed an orange piece of paper stuffed into the doorjamb. I yanked it out and held it between my thumb and index finger. One of my signs had been carefully torn into a small square so that only the word *Hunting* remained on it. Underneath, someone had scribbled *for you.*

Chapter 2

I was determined to replace the signs. This time, I'd make them myself. In the cabin, I pawed around the small extra bedroom that was a hodgepodge of storage. A flat cardboard mattress box stood upright between the bed and the wall. I hauled the cardboard out to the front lawn and spread it out. From my upstairs studio, I gathered several cans of paint and brushes.

Though it was early in the day, the sun was warm on my shoulders. But this time, I kept my shirt on. I wasn't taking any chances of someone finding me stripped to the waist again. After I cut the cardboard into nine-by-twelve-inch rectangles with a utility knife, I used a wide brush to coat each piece with black paint. They dried quickly, and by the time I finished applying black paint to the last one, the first pieces were dry enough to be lettered. With a smaller brush, I printed in bright orange: *Keep Out. No Trespassing or Hunting.* It felt damn satisfying to write the message over and over again.

When I finished lettering, I stood back and looked at the signs laid out on the grass. They would do just fine. But they needed to be waterproofed. I went into the cabin to find some plastic sheeting. In the small bedroom, I dragged a roll of clear plastic from under the bed.

Outside on the lawn, I covered each sign, wrapping the plastic like a bed sheet, tucking over the corners on the back, and stapling them down. Once they were protected by plastic, I gathered up the signs and carried them into the woodshed behind my cabin. At some point, I'd have to find time to walk my property again and nail the damn signs right back where they were before.

My plans were delayed by a message from my agent, so I never did get a chance to post the new signs. Riley Burns called to let me know that he'd had a request from a dealer in New York for a Samantha Warren original. I painted with acrylics, and my style was a cross between representational painting and expressionism, employing unexpected applications of color. My work was popular with certain buyers.

I decided to title this piece "The Artist at her Easel" and restrict my colors to the red and blue ranges. With a large mirror in my studio, I used myself as a model: the artist standing with brush in hand, a palette of paints in the foreground, the back of an easel framing one edge of the canvas. After a couple of weeks of uninterrupted work, the painting was finished, and after it dried for a few days, I drove to Clayton to ship it to the dealer.

Miss Helen, the postmistress, was used to me bringing in packages to be shipped. I think she liked it when I brought in a package because that meant I had to linger longer at the counter while she figured the postage. "What's it of this time, dear?" she asked, always curious about my paintings.

"Me," I said.

"Oh!" She put her hand to her chest. "How lovely."

She probably wouldn't think the painting was lovely if she saw it. She probably wouldn't understand it. In my work, I employed distortion just enough so that the viewer recognizes the subject matter but senses that something's askew. That blurring of reality and my unconventional use of color did not make for the realistic painting that I'm sure Miss Helen imagined.

As I drove back up Hurricane Mountain, I felt relaxed, glad to have the painting done and in the mail. With the top off the Jeep, the breeze ruffled my short hair. The radio blared Cher's, "*I Believe,*" and I sang along to it.

As I neared my property line, I caught a glimpse of a torn piece of orange paper hanging from a pine tree. Just seeing it and remembering how someone had torn down my signs jerked me out of my relaxed mood. I'd have to make sure to get those new signs posted before summer was over and hunting season approached.

The previous fall, I'd put up with a few hunters straggling

through my property: Bernice and her son-in-law, a few men I knew from Jean's store. But I'd shivered every time I heard a gunshot, and I dreaded the possibility of more hunters. In my mind, I saw droves of people in orange, toting rifles, intruding on my safe haven. The truth was, not only did I not want strangers on my land, I hated guns. Firearms were foreign to me. Owning guns seemed natural to everyone else around here, though. Jean kept a rifle at her cabin and a handgun at the store in case she needed protection. And it seemed that nearly everyone in western Maine owned at least one hunting rifle.

I was tired of fighting with Jean, tired of worrying about whoever had torn down the signs on my property. In the afternoon, after painting all morning, I drove down to the state park on Lake Rand just to clear my mind. At the park entrance, a ranger waved me through the gate, and I turned into the parking lot. The pine-canopied campground was full of activity, jammed with RVs and tents. I grabbed my towel bag and a blanket and walked the path to the beach. It was a spectacular afternoon—the blue sky embracing a hot sun.

The beach was crowded with people in swimsuits, looking to cool off on a hot mid-June afternoon. Mothers and a few dads watched their young children building sandcastles at the water's edge. Older children and some adults swam or floated on tubes. A group of teenagers sat farther out on a canvas-covered raft, swinging their feet in the water.

I was lucky to find a semi-secluded spot on the sand where I could spread my plaid stadium blanket. I lay facedown on the blanket and dozed in the sun. When I awoke, rivulets of sweat were running under my knees and between my breasts. Rolling over, I sat up, hugged my knees, and watched a chipmunk scurry from a picnic area to a grove of pine trees. The chipmunk was carrying a crust of bread in its mouth. The tops of tents were visible beyond the day picnicking area. The beach seemed even busier now as campers drifted over from the tenting area for an afternoon swim. With the sun beating down on my shoulders, my back felt hot and tight. *Damn, I'm getting a burn.* Digging out a tube of suntan lotion from my beach bag, I began applying it to my arms. As I reached for my shoulders, I heard a familiar voice. "Need some help?"

I swung my head around and saw Kate Henley standing behind me. My heart began to race. "What a surprise. I didn't expect to see you here today."

"Why not? It's a great day for the beach."

I shaded my eyes to get a better look at her. The lovely lines of her long, lean body, outlined in a neon pink bathing suit, stunned me. "Are you enjoying your summer off from teaching?"

"Well, it's not really time off. I'm working on a research project." Kate was an assistant professor of women's history at Fredericksville College. I'd met her a few months earlier in the spring when the college had hung an exhibit of my paintings. There had been an immediate spark between us, but we hadn't run into each other since.

"Oh. Then shouldn't you be busy researching, your head buried in a computer or a book or something?"

"I hit a block in my writing and needed to get away from it to clear my thinking. I'm renting a cottage for the summer at Lake Rand, so I decided to come over here to the beach for the afternoon," she said. "What are you doing here, Samantha? Shouldn't you be making a painting or something?" Her gray eyes lit up when she smiled. With her bare toe, she kicked a little sand at me.

"Look." I held up my paint-stained fingers. "I worked all morning from the crack of dawn."

"Well, then, you deserve a break." Kneeling on my blanket, Kate grabbed the tube of lotion from my hand. I shivered when she began rubbing the tops of my shoulders, working the lotion into my skin. I was very aware of the pressure of her hands on my neck, rubbing lotion at the edge of my hairline. I was embarrassed to hear myself moan.

Kate squeezed more lotion into the cup of her palm. The lotion was cool at first on my skin, but her touch was like a flame, its warmth different from the sun's heat. Lightly, her fingers moved across my shoulders, the shoulder blades, the spine, moving in circles across my back. I felt myself growing dizzy, so I rested my head on my knees. When she tapped my arm, I quickly opened my eyes. Taking the tube from her, I began to twist the cap on, but she put her hand over mine to stop me.

"Could you do me first?" She stretched out belly down on my blanket, rolling her towel into a pillow. The long slope of her bare back mesmerized me. After a moment, she turned her head and glanced over at me. "Well?"

I slid closer and squeezed lotion into my palm, then rubbed my hands together. Timidly, I reached out and touched her arm, her skin sleek under my fingers. She sighed and closed her eyes. I rubbed lotion onto first one arm, then reached across to the other. I coated the back of her neck, where her short black hair ended in wisps. Then her shoulders, more lotion, down her lovely back, all the way down to the edge of the pink bathing suit. Kate's voice was muffled from lying facedown on the blanket. "Great," she said. "How about my legs?"

Scooting farther down on the blanket, I squeezed more lotion into my hands. Beginning at the feet, I massaged the skin around her anklebones. Pressing down, I worked my hands up her calves, feeling the firm muscle. When I hesitated just below her knees, she mumbled, "Go on."

I placed my hands on the back of her thighs and rubbed gently, my fingers light. I moved from the knee, slowly toward the elastic of her suit. Then shyly moved toward the inner thigh. I felt her quiver under my fingertips. I didn't want to stop, but a man and woman were strolling along the shoreline with two little kids who kept skipping in and out of the water. They were headed in our direction. Reluctantly, I pulled my hands away and sat back on my heels.

Kate rolled her head to look at me. She smiled, her eyelids heavy. "Thanks. Now I won't have to worry about getting skin cancer."

I stowed the lotion into my bag. Lying down on the blanket, the length of my body just barely touching hers, I was aware of her radiating heat.

After a while, Kate raised up on her elbows. "Want to swim?"

she asked. "It might cool us off."

"I'm not sure I want to cool off." I grinned.

Kate pushed up onto her knees and tossed her towel at me. "Come on," she called as she darted toward the water, sand spitting up from her feet. I admired the tight lines of her body in the pink bathing suit. Swinging her arms wide, she ran into the lake. After hesitating for a moment, she surface dove, disappearing and reappearing like a dolphin.

I jumped up and ran in after her. The water was deliciously cool on my feet, my ankles, my calves. As I waded deeper in, the shock of its coldness hit me. I began to breaststroke. She seemed far away from me, and I beaded in on her. When I got closer, she swam off again. I followed, glimpsing her sleek body under the water, the flutter kick of her feet. She reached the floating raft and hefted herself up the ladder. I placed my hand on the raft near her feet, and she dove over me, the water breaking around her, splashing my head and shoulders. Again she was gone.

Again I followed, this time to the right, away from the other swimmers. She waited for me, treading water. I swam up beside her and she flicked water at me with her hand, laughing. Then she surface dove, and I lost track of her until I felt her fingers on my legs, lightly caressing my thighs like sea grass. She surfaced then a few feet in front of me and started swimming toward shore. I watched her go, fed up with her game. This was like trying to catch a fish with your bare hands. The minute you think you've got a grasp, it slips between your fingers.

As soon as Kate had swum in far enough for her feet to touch the lake's sandy bottom, she stopped, turned around, and waved for me. It didn't take me long to join her. We stood neck deep, our faces inches from each other, our bodies concealed by water, the mountains rising up around us.

Still in my wet swimsuit, I drove up the gravel road that scaled Hurricane Mountain. All around me was the lush thick green of June. The oak, maple, and birch trees made a canopy through which the sunlight dappled onto the road. Phlox grew in lavender and pink patches, and wild daisies seemed to line the road for miles. The wooden bridge over the brook gave just a little under the weight of my Jeep, and I looked down at the clear water gushing under the bridge.

As I neared the top of the mountain, I was relieved that I didn't see any sign of Bernice. When I passed her camp, it looked closed up and her car was not parked in front of it. Across from Bernice's, on the other side of the road, ran an old stone wall spotted with moss and lichen. Near the opening, marked by two granite posts, I turned onto the lane that led to my cabin and Jean's.

I swung into my yard and shut off the motor. Quickly, I changed out of my suit and tossed my wet towel onto a hook on the bathroom wall. In the living room, I sank into the futon, kicking off my sneakers. Outside the picture window, a few cirrus clouds were wafting over the mountain range. I watched them shift in shape as my fantasies drifted to Kate Henley.

"Samantha? Are you home?"

Kate's voice from the foot of the stairs interrupted my absorption in my painting. I'd been working at a project non-stop for nearly a week and lost all sense of time or the outside world. I shook my head to clear it. "I'm up here. Come on up."

She climbed the spiral staircase to the loft. I raised my hand and waved hello as I set my brush on the gutter of the easel. Looking at my paint-stained fingers, Kate said, "Oh, you're working. Keep on with it. I'll come back another time."

"No, no. Stay. I should leave this alone for a while anyway." I pointed to a canvas propped on the easel. "I need to freshen up, then we'll find something to eat."

"You've forgotten, haven't you?" Kate said. "About lunch."

I felt my cheeks redden. "Of course not." Over the weekend, I'd run into Kate at the Book Barn when we were both buying a Sunday *New York Times*. We'd had hazelnut coffee and cinnamon scones at the Bakery Hut, and I remembered now that I'd invited her for lunch. I don't know how it could have slipped my mind.

In the kitchen, I had trouble finding something to serve her. I pulled pita bread, Gouda cheese, bean sprouts, a tomato, and brown mustard from the refrigerator. If it was obvious to Kate that I was improvising, she didn't let on. Instead, she set to work helping to make the sandwiches. "That's a cute picture on the fridge," she said as she sliced cheese.

"My nephew Timmy drew it—my brother's boy. He's quite a little artist for an eight-year-old, don't you think?"

"Must take after his aunt."

We ate at the small pine table near the window that looked out over the meadow. Kate filled me in on the article she was writing, and I told her a little about the painting I was doing. While we lingered over tea, I told her about the deer that often came to my yard in the mornings or evenings. Pointing out the window, I said, "He feeds on grass, and I love watching him."

After we finished our tea and cleared the table of dishes, I suggested we take a walk. I guided her across the meadow to an old logging road. Deerflies were buzzing and the birds were making their notes of music, but otherwise it was still and quiet on the mountain.

"Is all of this your property?" Kate made a sweeping gesture with her hand.

I looked out over the mountainside: the wild green fields, the mighty pine and spruce, granite boulders jutting from the ribs of the earth. "My land starts back near the stone fence along the gravel road where you drove in. It stretches a long way down there." I pointed into the distance toward a steep slope below us. "Jean McCray's property runs parallel to mine. Her cabin isn't far from mine, beyond it and to the side. From my front step, I can just see her roof through the trees."

"I met her at The Village Store. She owns it, doesn't she?" Kate pulled a long piece of grass and chewed the sweet end.

"Yeah, and she practically lives in that store this time of year. With tourist season, she's up to her eyeballs with running that place."

"I know what you mean," Kate said. "I've been stopping in there pretty regularly since I've been renting the cottage. Anytime I go to pick up milk or something, no matter what time of day or night, Jean seems to be there."

Suddenly, there was a raucous flurry of wings, and a partridge flew up from the underbrush. Both of us jumped, startled at the loud swoosh. "Oh," Kate gasped, putting her hand to her throat.

"Shh," I whispered. "We'll probably flush out more birds. A lot of them nest in this grove of trees."

Kate dropped her hand, recovered from her fright. She spit out the chewed piece of grass and visored her eyes in an attempt to see the partridge, which had flown off. "Must be good hunting here in the fall."

I still hadn't gotten around to hanging the new signs, but I told her, "I'm going to post my land against hunting."

Kate raised her eyebrows. "That will make you popular around here. Hunting's as much of the culture as beans and hot dogs on Saturday night."

"Tell me about it. In November, orange is a fashion statement." I laughed, then said, "It was different in Rhode Island. If we saw guns, it meant a robbery was going on and someone was likely to get hurt."

"Here, every boy and a lot of girls get a rifle when they turn twelve. They treasure that twenty-two, and it's a mark of passage when they go on their first hunt. It has to do with heritage and tradition."

"It's all new to me. Last fall was my first year on the mountain during bird and deer seasons. I don't like guns, and right away, I knew I didn't want anyone hunting here. But I gave in and let my neighbor Bernice Slade come onto my property. She argued that she and her husband had always hunted on this piece of land, free and clear, and his father before them."

"And I suppose his father before him."

I nodded. "But I didn't feel comfortable about it. I'm not going to allow her or anyone else onto my land with a gun ever again." An image of the stranger sneaking up on me unawares ran through my mind and sent a shiver down my back.

"Have you broken the news to your neighbor?"

"I don't know if she knows yet or not." I thought of the signs that had been ripped down. "I don't see why it should be a big deal. She's got the rest of Hurricane Mountain to hunt. Come on. I've got a treat for you." I led her down the hill to the spring.

19

The spring welled up from an underground stream that ran down the mountain. It was simply a hole in the ground, ringed with rocks and protected by a wooden circular cover. I knelt, lifted the cover by its handle, and cleared a few leaves from the surface of the spring. The water was so clear, we could see down into its dark heart. "This is the best water in the world." I scooped some with my cupped hands and sipped, then wiped my mouth with the back of my hand. "You've got to try it."

Kate squatted down and scooped a handful of water to her mouth. "Um, cold." She smiled. "And delicious. You're right, it's the best I've ever tasted." Kate sighed, sitting back on her heels. Little beads of water clung to her upper lip, and impulsively, I reached over and wiped her mouth with my fingertips. She held my hand there, pressed against the wet flesh of her lips. I was still kneeling, so I leaned in to kiss her. Just as our mouths met, I lost my balance, knocking us both backward. "Were you trying to push me into the spring?" Kate laughed as we stood up and wiped pieces of dried leaf from our clothes.

To hide my embarrassment, I suggested we fill our water bottles. Then we continued hiking until we came to the Bailey field, an abandoned farm owned many years before by a family named—what else?—Bailey. Birds flew in and out of apple trees that were in varying stages of neglect, and the air was thick with the sound of *chick-a-dee-dee*. Near the old orchard, an open cellar hole marked the spot where there had once been a house. There was no trace of the house anymore, though a rectangular gap measured the perimeters of what once had stood there. Crevices in the granite walls of the cellar were filled in now with moss and weeds. I jumped down onto the packed dirt floor and motioned for Kate to follow. Inside the old cellar hole, we scouted around, examining little things we found, like an amber-colored glass bottle and a porcelain doorknob. I watched Kate intently searching for clues of the history of the place and of the families who had once lived there. An image of the two of us leaning against the granite wall in an embrace flashed through my mind, and I yearned to take her in my arms. But after my fiasco at the spring, I felt foolish and let the moment go.

When it was time to leave the cellar hole, I made a step for Kate by lacing my hands together and boosted her out. Once Kate was on higher elevation, she reached down and offered her hand. I took it and pulled myself up. When I was standing, Kate didn't let go of my hand. She took my other hand, and we leaned into each other, our foreheads touching. I think the birds held their songs for a few moments because all I could hear was our breathing as it sped up and mingled. I closed my eyes and took in her earthy scent, a smell of musk and sweetness. Then she let go.

As we started to leave, she said, "What's that shiny thing on the ground?"

In the grass, I spotted a spent cartridge and knelt down to pick it up. "This isn't very old," I said, examining it. "From a rifle, I think. Looks like it hasn't been here long." As I got to my feet, I stuffed the brass casing into my pocket.

We hiked on farther, making a circle so that eventually we ended up on the gravel road that led back to my log cabin. On the other side of the road, Bernice was coming out of a wooden shed next to her cabin, carrying a can of paint.

Bernice and I had not had much to do with each other in the year I'd lived on the mountain. There wasn't any real reason for me not to like her. But we were definitely from different worlds. It was clear that she saw me as an outsider, a woman who didn't know a thing about living on the mountain—and didn't belong here. For my part, I thought she was an alcoholic hussy. I always went out of my way to keep my distance from her.

"Who's that?" Kate whispered.

"The neighbor I was telling you about," I whispered back.

Standing at a cedar picnic table, Bernice was prying open the paint can and hadn't seemed to notice us. There was an empty pint-size bottle of vodka lying on its side on the table.

"Hey, Bernice, what are you up to?" I called.

Looking up and spotting us, Bernice set the cover back onto the paint can and walked over to the roadside. When she came closer, I noticed her nose and cheeks were flushed, and I figured she'd been into the vodka. "I'm fixing up the old camp. I kind of let it go after my husband died. Now I plan to spruce it up." She patted her hair, which was dyed an orangey blond and teased. "You out for a walk?"

"Just getting some exercise," I explained. "And showing Kate around."

She slapped a mosquito on her arm, then flicked it off her skin with a painted fingernail. "Pretty up here, isn't it?" she said to Kate. "I spend as much time here as I can." Her words slurred a little.

"Yes, it's beautiful."

"Are you from around here?" she asked Kate.

"I'm renting a cottage on Lake Rand for the summer."

"Well, we'll probably run into each other again sometime." Then she turned to me. "Samantha, you're not planning on posting your land, are you? I could swear I saw some pieces of signs on a few trees."

"We'll talk about it another time," I said. "Right now Kate and I have to be going." I took Kate's arm, and we walked briskly along the road. I could feel Bernice's eyes on our backs. At the double granite posts, we turned off the gravel road.

"You don't like her, do you?" Kate said as we walked down the lane toward my cabin.

"We just don't see eye to eye. But then, I don't know her very well."

Kate opened her car door and stood with her hand on the latch. "Thanks for lunch and the walk." She climbed into the car and pulled the door closed. Then through the open window, she added, "Stop by the next time you get down to Clayton."

"You're sure it wouldn't disturb your writing?"

She smiled. "If it were you, I wouldn't consider it a disruption."

As I watched her drive away, I stuck my hand into my pocket and curled my fingers around the spent bullet casing we'd found near the abandoned cellar hole.

Chapter 3

As usual, it was after ten p.m. before Jean got back to her cabin from the store. Seeing that my lights were still on, she tooted the truck horn as she passed. That meant I should go to her cabin for a nightcap, so I walked over with a flashlight showing the path. We sat out on her deck in green canvas chairs, our feet propped up on the railing. Badger lay next to us, his head resting on outstretched paws.

The stars at night on Hurricane Mountain were remarkable. The onyx sky was absolutely dotted with them. We were chatting about a woman Jean had met that day at the store at lunchtime. "She's a game warden for the state. The tag on her shirt read *Ranger Hillby*. While I was wrapping an Italian sandwich for her, I pointed to her name tag and asked, 'Is there a first name with that?' She looked me in the eyes and said, 'It's Amy,' and held out her hand for me to shake." Jean took a swig of her beer and sighed. "I think I'm in love."

"Don't rush into anything," I said, remembering the times she'd been disappointed by romantic relationships when we were in college together. During those days at RISD, I'd known Jean to be dumped a few times and cheated on more than once, and I didn't want her to get hurt again.

"Well, I'll see if she comes into the store again. She's stationed in the Clayton area for the summer," Jean said, then changed the subject abruptly. She went into a long saga about her day. In the middle of the afternoon, she'd had a whole family come in. "Scads of kids. They were everywhere, fingering everything on the shelves."

"See, that's why I'm glad I don't have kids," I said. "They're always into everything. Just can't leave things alone. That's exactly why I like being an aunt instead of a mother—I can spend time with Timmy when I want to, then take him back to my brother's house."

Jean ignored my comment and went on with her story. "Finally, the dad pays for a bag of pretzels and they troop out, one by one. Gets to the last kid, and I see a trail of something on the floor as he reaches the door. 'Just a minute,' I yell at him. He darts out the door, but I'm right behind him. Come to find out, the kid's got ice cream bars stuffed in his pants pockets. The damn stuff is melting and dripping from his pants leg. Then I see that all the kids have something bulging in their pockets. A Mars candy bar is sticking out of one girl's shorts. Another kid's got a small bag of Doritos in the back pocket of his swimming trunks. 'Hey, what the hell do you think you're doing?' I say. But by then, the parents are already waiting inside this broken-down station wagon, and the engine's running. The dad's got the doors open on one side, and the mother's got the doors open on the other side. The kids scramble in, and they peel out of the parking lot. Nearly hit an SUV that was pulling in."

We were laughing about her story when, out of the blue, Jean brought up the issue of the *No Hunting* signs. "I'm glad you listened to reason and decided not to post new signs, Sam. I mean, it was a really dumb-ass idea in the first place." She chuckled as if I must think it was dumb, too.

"I am going to hang new signs. I just haven't gotten around to it."

When Jean's feet hit the deck floor, Badger raised his head. Jean set her can of Miller Lite on the railing and swung around to face me. "Are you nuts? You saw what happened the first time. Someone got mad and yanked them all down. It'll just happen again. Locals don't like the idea of private land on this mountain. They don't want to be shut out of land they've always hunted. Bernice thinks it's a bad idea, too."

"I've made up my mind. I'm going to do it before hunting season comes."

"Just because some stranger scares you out of your wits when you're parading around outside half-naked, you think you've got to keep everyone away."

"It's not just that. I don't like to see innocent animals slaughtered." Even I could hear the prissy sound of my voice.

"Good goddamn!" Jean snapped. "You come up here from the big city. Think those pretty deer and birds are nature's gift to you alone in your own little paradise. Got some idealistic idea about not killing animals, not eating meat. That is so seventies, Sam. Give it up."

I twisted the cap onto my empty bottle of water. "Look, I believe what I believe. I have to do what's right for me."

"And put two centuries of tradition on its ear. And probably put me out of business in the process." Jean threw her head back and drained her beer. Then she stood up, nearly knocking over the canvas chair. "I'm going to bed. You can sit out here and dream your silly, hippy dreams, but some of us have to go to work in the morning. Come on, Badger." As she stomped off, the dog at her heels, I could hear the crunch of the beer can in her hand. There were noises from inside the cabin: the sink running, the toilet flushing, Badger moving around. Then the lights went out, and I was left sitting in total darkness. I snapped on my flashlight, and under the sky of stars, walked home.

The summer tourist season was in full swing. I knew that Jean was very busy at the store, so again I offered to lend a hand. A few days after our spat on her back deck, I drove down to Clayton and arrived in time for the late afternoon shift. Grabbing a clean white apron from under the counter, I slipped it over my head. I pivoted a little so Jean could tie the strings. "Thanks for helping out," she said gruffly as she pulled the strings tight and gave them a little tug.

Just then, a customer came in and ordered a pizza. I quickly got to work spreading sauce, cheese, and pepperoni on the dough. By the time I slid the pizza into the oven, Jean had left to take Badger to the vet for his annual check-up. I watched her red truck back out of the parking lot, Badger's head sticking out the passenger side window. I'd told her that I'd cover for her so she could get some errands done and go home early. Jean had scheduled a high school boy, Robby Blackstone, to come in at 4:45, and the two of us would close the store at the end of the shift.

Fifteen minutes hadn't passed when a blond game warden came through the screen door. She moved in an athletic way, carrying her body with confidence. Her square face was topped by a punk hairstyle, standing on end with bangs that hung over her forehead. Her name tag read *Ranger Hillby*. She came up to the counter and ordered an Italian sandwich, and while I was making it, I noticed how she kept glancing around as if she were searching for someone. Finally, she asked, "Jean around?"

"You just missed her." I handed her the sandwich. "Should I tell her you were looking for her?"

"No, that's all right. Thanks." She took the bag with the sandwich and a can of cranberry juice and walked out the screen door.

Later, I was at the back of the store, checking stock in the soda cooler when the bell over the front door jangled, then the screen door slammed. "Robby, can you get that?" I called. When he didn't answer, I realized he'd probably taken the trash out to the bin behind the store. Setting a liter bottle of soda on the shelf, I closed the cooler door and headed up front to see what the customer wanted. Halfway up the narrow aisle, I stopped. Standing at the magazine rack was the man who had surprised me on the mountain: Garret Belling. He hadn't spotted me yet, but I had no choice. I had to wait on him. "Can I help you?" I asked tersely as I slipped behind the counter. He'd been thumbing through a *Farmer's Almanac*, which he casually set back in the rack as he stared deliberately at my breasts. I felt exposed.

"Do you need something?" I asked, my voice even icier than before.

His grin was wide and slow, carving a path across his face. He brought his eyes up to meet mine, and I blushed. He knew I was uncomfortable, and he was enjoying every minute of it. "Cigarettes," he said, pointing to the display behind me. "Carton of Camels."

I swung around, furious at myself for the flush that I could feel burning my cheeks. Just as I reached toward the cigarette display, another customer came into the store. I heard the two greet each other as if they had been acquaintances for some time. I recognized that voice, too. Bernice Slade. "You two know each other?" I asked, turning around to face them and placing the carton of Camels on the counter.

"Garret works at the mill," Bernice said. "He's been asking questions about Hurricane Mountain. I invited him up to give the fishing a try since he's been showing a little bit of interest in this area."

More than a little bit. I remembered the way Garret had appraised my cabin and land with his calculating eye.

"We're going to see if we can catch some brook trout," Bernice said.

They looked odd together. Bernice was older by at least fifteen years; her brassy hair was wildly teased, and she was wearing pink knit pants and top. Her sneakers were dotted with sequins, topped by hot pink socks. Garret, glancing around the store furtively, was dressed in a faded black Grateful Dead shirt, black jeans, and military boots.

Straightening the pink visor on her head, Bernice said, "What else do we need, Garret, before we head up to the brook?"

"A few cold ones. We'll want to wet the whistle." Garret cupped his hand and brought it to his mouth, mimicking the act of drinking. He looked at me as he wiped his mouth with his knuckles.

"Can't forget that," Bernice agreed, looking as if she'd had a few already. "A six-pack okay?" She turned to walk back toward the beer cooler.

"Make it a twelve-pack. Budweiser," Garret called after her. He never offered to get it himself. Choosing a disposable butane lighter from the display, he placed it on the counter next to the carton of cigarettes. "That's a nice piece of land you own. Don't suppose there's any chance you've changed your mind about selling?"

A rush of anger hit me at his bringing up the subject again when I'd been emphatic about not ever wanting to sell. I didn't like him to see the effect he had on me, so I ignored him.

He leaned on the counter and bent his head toward me. He smelled like beer and cigarette smoke. "By the way, what did you say your name was?"

"I didn't." I gave him a cutting look as I placed the cigarettes and lighter in a paper bag. "And you didn't say you were a friend of Bernice's that day you trespassed on my property."

"Trespass? That's a hard choice of words for someone who was taking an innocent stroll. I was just casually exploring the mountainside."

I was about to make a smart comeback when Bernice returned with a twelve-pack of Budweiser. "That'll be it, I guess. No, wait, Samantha. Wrap us up a wedge of sharp cheese, too."

"Samantha," Garret repeated softly, and I shuddered when I heard my name on his lips.

We had a steady stream of customers who kept Robby and me running all evening. By 8:30, it had slowed down enough so that we could prepare for closing. After Robby wiped down the pizza station and swept the floor, I told him he could leave early.

Just before I locked up, Sarah Nelson came into the store. She kept a camper on Lake Rand, commuted daily to Fredericksville to her job, and was a regular customer in the summer. "How are things at the mill?" I asked as I bagged her bread, Rice Krispies, and carton of milk.

"There are rumors about going on strike. Everyone's pissed that our health premiums went up and we didn't get a cost-of-living raise." Sarah picked up a *Fredericksville Journal* and handed it to me.

I folded the newspaper, slipped it into the brown paper bag, and punched in fifty cents on the cash register. "Think there'll be one? A strike?"

"I hope not." Sarah zipped open a wallet that was bulging with pictures of her kids. "The last one got really nasty. That was in 1987, long before you moved here. Mill workers were packing handguns and threatening to use them. It lasted sixteen months, and people were feeling pretty hopeless by the time the strike was called off. Families lost their homes. People took sides, management against labor, strikers against scabs. It split up lifelong friends, relatives. Even brothers, like Mike and Johnny Allen. They both went on strike with the union, then Johnny got desperate for money and broke the lines. Mike won't speak to him to this day."

"What a mess," I said. "I hope it doesn't come to that again."

"I don't think it will. Nobody dares strike when the economy's this bad. With jobs going overseas these days, what I'm more afraid of is the mill shutting down, then we'd be out of jobs altogether." The screen door banged open and a small boy dressed in pajamas came in, his bare feet padding along the wood floor. He ran to his mother and wrapped himself around her leg. Sarah patted his head absently as she handed me a ten-dollar bill. I broke her ten and gave her change. "Do you know a guy named Garret Belling? Works at the mill, friend of Bernice's."

She took the change and zipped her wallet. "Oh, I don't think he's really Bernice's friend. They hardly see each other. Garret works out on the floor on the paper machines with Bernice's son-in-law, and she's in the office in bookkeeping."

"Well, they were in here together tonight. Bernice was taking Garret fishing."

"Then Garret must have weaseled an invitation from her." She looked me in the eye. "He's trouble."

I started to tell her about the run-in with Garret, but the little boy in pajamas, still wrapped around her leg, began to whine.

Sarah carried her bag of groceries to the door, the boy following close behind. Just before she went out, she turned to me. "I wouldn't trust Garret Belling. If he's poking around, that means he's up to no good. Watch your back around him."

"Well, thanks," I joked. "That makes me feel a whole lot better." But I felt a shudder at her warning.

Chapter 4

Ruby-throated hummingbirds were at the feeder again, fighting to be first in line for the sweet red water. I'd been paying close attention to the tiny green birds and had drawn many studies of them, which were now tacked up in my studio.

For most of the morning, I worked in my studio on a painting of a hummingbird approaching the bright red lips of a woman, a cube of sugar on the glistening flesh of her tongue. Even though it was hot and stuffy in the loft, I pushed myself to continue working. My shoulders were aching when I stepped back to appraise my work. I had made good progress on the painting. When it was complete, I would ship it to a gallery in New Hampshire that was hanging an exhibit called "New Images of Nature."

But my plan was interrupted in a way that would change the entire course of my life.

At noon that day, I took a break from painting and walked down to the stream behind my cabin. Sitting on the bank, I dangled my feet in the cold water for a while, listening to the birds singing. When I got back to the cabin, the answering machine on my phone was beeping, but I ignored it while I made lunch. When I finally pressed the button, my sandwich leaking mayonnaise onto the machine, the mechanical voice said, "You have two messages." I wasn't paying much attention, as I was busy wolfing down the sandwich. I ripped a piece of bread with my teeth, but in the middle of chewing it, something on the machine caught my attention. I swallowed too quickly, and the bread got stuck in my throat. It took several gulps of Snapple to dislodge it. With a mayonnaise-smeared finger, I pushed the replay button. The first message was from my dentist, reminding me of an appointment. I pushed *skip* to get to the second message. The sound was garbled, but the voice sounded like my mother's. I replayed it several times, turning up the volume on the machine.

Thirty minutes after hearing the message, I was in my Jeep racing toward Providence.

As I drove, I called Kate and told her what had happened and that I was going home for a few days to be with my mother. The cell phone connection was amazingly clear. "What can I do to help?" she asked right away.

"Nothing, really. I might call you from my mother's if I need a friend to talk to. Is that okay?"

"Of course, Sam. Call anytime, day or night."

Next, I called Jean at the store and told her about my brother. She'd met Dan a few times when he came to our art exhibits at RISD. Unflappable Jean was shocked at the news. "My God, I can't believe it."

"I can't either. Look, I'll be at my mother's for at least a week, I think. Will you pick up my mail for me at the post office? And keep an eye on my cabin—make sure no one is nosing around there."

"Are you worried that Garret guy might come back?"

I rolled down the window as I slowed for the tollbooth in Lewiston. "I think it's best to be on the lookout for anything suspicious," I said before I hung up.

Once I passed through the tollbooth onto Interstate 95, I set the Jeep on cruise and allowed myself to think about what had happened and what would be facing me in Providence. My brother Dan was dead. I could hardly take in the news. His wife, Jennifer, too. Both of them not even forty yet, gone, just like that. I didn't know the details. My mother was too shaken to explain much over the phone, except that they had been in a car accident on their way to work. Dan and Jennifer had jobs in computer technology in separate offices along the Interstate 95 corridor, and they took that commute to work every weekday. It was a busy highway, especially during commuter hours. The first thing I'd asked my mother was if Timmy was all right. I was overcome with relief when she'd told me that he had not been in the car with his parents.

My mind was a jumble of memories as I scooted around Boston's busy traffic and continued on 95 toward Rhode Island. Seeing the exit signs for Foxborough reminded me of the time Dan and I took Timmy to a New England Patriots game. Timmy was five then and excited beyond himself. He wore a Patriots jersey under his fall jacket, and I had to keep reminding him to zip up so he wouldn't get cold. He wanted everyone to see his new jersey. Dan and I let him order whatever he wanted from the vendors, and he noshed his way through hot dogs, chips, cotton candy, and Pepsi. On the way home after the game, we had to pull over onto the shoulder of the road so Timmy could throw up. But I never saw such a grin on his face as when he wiped the froth from his mouth.

When I crossed the state line from Massachusetts to Rhode Island, I slowed the Jeep, barely going the speed limit. As I neared Providence, more and more, I dreaded going home. I knew my mother would be a wreck and would be counting on me to help her get through this. And what in the world was going to happen to Timmy?

My mother's small house in the Mount Pleasant neighborhood was surrounded by wood tenement buildings. The house hadn't changed in the thirty-seven years she'd lived there, except now there was a heavy chill hanging over the tiny rooms. Grief made the house feel dank.

Kneeling on her kitchen linoleum, I was the same height as my eight-year-old nephew. How was I going to tell him that in one moment, his whole life had changed and that from now on, nothing would ever be the same? "Timmy," I said, "look at me." I took hold of his shoulders and turned him slightly so that he was facing me. "I want to talk to you about something."

"What, Aunt Sam?" he asked, twisting a button on the neck of his polo shirt. A thread was hanging from it.

As I faced my nephew, my mother sitting behind us at the table stunned by her own fresh grief, I thought how much I didn't want to be here. How I didn't want to deal with what was ahead of us. I wished I were on Hurricane Mountain, in the peaceful isolation of my cabin.

"Timmy." I took his chin in my hand and made him look at me. "We have to talk about something important. Mommy and Daddy aren't coming back."

"You mean I'm going to stay at Grandma's overnight?"

"It's more than that. Your parents were in a bad car accident." I hesitated, not wanting to put words to it. "Do you know what *die* means?"

His eyes opened wide, then he looked back to the floor. "Yeah."

"Well, your mommy and daddy died." I squeezed his shoulders gently. "Someone was going the wrong way on the highway and hit Mommy and Daddy's car."

"Why would someone be driving the wrong way? That's really stupid."

"The man must have entered the highway on the off-ramp. The police think he'd been drinking. That happens sometimes when a person drinks too much beer or wine or whiskey. They can't think straight, and they make bad mistakes, like hitting your parents' car."

"Mommy and Daddy weren't drinking beer."

"Of course not, they were on the way to work. The accident wasn't their fault. It was the man in the other car who made it happen. He'd been working on the night shift and when he got out of work, it was real early in the morning, still dark out. Most people were still sleeping. Instead of going home, the man went to a bar and got drunk. Then he drove his car when he shouldn't have."

"Should I be mad at him for what he did to Mommy and Daddy?"

"I know I am. I'm damn mad!" A jumble of emotions boiled up as I said those words. I was outraged about Dan's and Jennifer's senseless deaths. And I was ashamed for worrying about how this family tragedy might affect my own life. I bit down on my lower lip in an effort to get a grip on myself. "It's okay for you to be mad, too."

"Oh." His arms hung limply at his side, and he didn't seem sure how to react. After a pause he said, "What man crashed into my car? What's his name?"

"We can talk about that later. Right now I want to make sure you understand that Mommy and Daddy aren't ever coming back."

I tried to hug him, but he pushed away from me. "Why aren't they?"

This was even harder than I thought it would be. "I just told you, Timmy. They died."

My mother started muttering at the table, shaking her head. "This isn't happening," she mumbled. "Dan can't be dead. He was here just this morning when he dropped Timmy off." She wiped her face with a tissue. "I take care of Timmy the days he doesn't go to day camp. I told Dan I could take care of him every day, but he said no it was too much for me. Dan—he's such a sweetheart—he's been worried about me ever since I had that heart spell last winter. So I take Timmy just two days a week, Tuesday and Thursday, and the other days he goes to day camp. What day is it today?"

"Thursday, Mom," I reminded her.

"That's right. Thursday. After Dan dropped him off, Timmy and I baked cookies. I had a new recipe for butterscotch chip that I cut out of the paper." My mother dabbed her eyes with a tissue. "Remember, Timmy dear? We put some on a plate to save for Daddy. They're still there on the counter. 'See you later,' that's what he said when he dropped you off. 'Mommy and I will be back after work, Timmy. You be a good boy for Grandma.' Of course, your mother was sitting out in the car like always. Never could bother herself to come in."

Timmy, his face pale, ignored her as he concentrated on pulling a hangnail on his thumb.

My mother let out a huge sigh and directed her comments to me. "We baked those cookies first thing this morning, then next thing I knew, there's a police car in the driveway." My mother seemed to have a need to tell this story over and over again. I'd heard it countless times since I'd arrived a few hours earlier, but I listened as if it were the first time, thinking there might be some new detail I'd missed. "A woman officer shows up at the door. She had a funny name—Officer Knockers. I remember seeing it on her name tag and thinking it must be hard to go around with a name like that. And she called me by my first name. 'Margaret' she said, just like we were old friends, like I wasn't forty years older than her. Then she told me about the accident, and I wanted to slam the door in her face and make her get out." My mother wadded up the tissue and added it to the pile on the table. "Samantha, look at Timmy—he's just a little boy. How's he going to get by without a father? Who's going to teach him the things a father's supposed to teach his son? Like shaving. I can't be expected to show that boy how to use a razor."

"What's wrong with Grandma?" Timmy asked. "She's acting funny."

"She's just sad," I said. "That's why she's crying. It's okay to cry when you're sad, you know." Timmy shrugged. His own eyes were brimming with tears, but he wouldn't let them go. I patted him lightly on the head. "Why don't you watch TV for a little while before bedtime?"

That's all it took, a simple sign of dismissal. He dashed from the kitchen, through the archway, and into the living room. I had no idea if he really understood what had happened to his parents. I stood up and shook my legs to get the kinks out of my knees. My mother was sitting with her elbow on the table, her head resting on one hand. The pile of wet tissues had doubled. She stared out the window at the driveway as if she expected Dan to open the door at any moment. I scooped up the dirty tissues and threw them into the wastebasket.

Chapter 5

I had my hands full tying up Dan and Jennifer's financial loose ends: getting the death certificates, filing a claim for the life insurance, settling the hospital bill, contacting Social Security so Timmy would get SSI. And I had to get Dan and Jennifer's house cleaned out and ready to sell. They had renovated an old Victorian in the Armory district, and I figured it would sell quickly once it was on the market, but first I had to find a Realtor to list it. When these things were taken care of and my mother was strong enough to be alone, I could get back to Hurricane Mountain. A week, maybe, if I was lucky. A week to get back to my own work.

The next day, my uncle and aunt were coming from Westerly on the other side of the state to take Timmy back with them. My mother's youngest brother and his wife had two children of their own, but only Juliet, a senior in high school, was still at home. My cousin Chris had an apartment with some other women outside of Boston. She was a bio-ethics student at Brandeis and was working hard with summer classes and a part-time job. When Uncle Bill and Aunt Millie called on Friday and offered to have Timmy live with them—Chris's room was empty anyway and they missed having kids around—to tell the truth, I jumped at the chance. My mother wasn't so sure, but I convinced her that it would be best for Timmy. It really was a good solution all around. There was no way my mother could handle taking care of him on a full-time basis, and I certainly wasn't going to take him back to Hurricane Mountain with me. I had no room in my life for a child. He'd be best off with Uncle Bill and Aunt Millie.

The phone rang. I couldn't find the portable until the fourth ring. It was on the kitchen counter, covered with newspaper clippings of Dan's and Jennifer's obituaries. When I picked up the phone, I heard Uncle Bill's voice on the other end.

"How's Margaret?" he asked, and I told him my mother was exhausted after the funeral but managing to hold on.

I waited for him to tell me what time to expect him and Aunt Millie the next day. But instead he said, "We've got a snag here in our plans, Samantha. It's not going to work out for us to pick up Timmy tomorrow. Christine has mono, and we're driving to Boston and bringing her home until she recovers."

My mother was mouthing words to me—something like *who is it*? I wagged my hand at her and said into the phone, "I'm really sorry to hear that, Uncle Bill. Is Chris terribly sick?"

"Mostly worn out. She can hardly put one foot in front of the other, she's so weak. A month or so of rest here at home will do her a world of good. Her mother will fatten her up with home-cooking and spoil her with pampering." He paused, and I could hear the phone line buzzing. Then he added what I was dreading to hear: "This mono could be contagious. I don't think it'd be wise to chance Timmy catching it."

A month? What were we going to do with Timmy during that time? I had to get back to Hurricane Mountain, and my mother was in desperate need of rest herself.

Just before my uncle hung up, he said, "We'll reassess things after Christine gets well. I'll be in touch with you." What did that mean, I wondered. Were they planning on taking Timmy or not?

"That was Bill? What did he want?" my mother asked. When I told her what he'd said, she spread her hands on the table and whimpered, "What else can go wrong?"

I was too shaken by my uncle's call to respond. I avoided her eyes as I placed the phone on its base.

"I should try to keep Timmy here," my mother said. "That's what Dan would want. Timmy's used to my house, and he could just move into Dan's old room."

That would be an easy solution, but I knew it wouldn't work. "Mom," I said, turning and facing her, "we've been over this already. Think about it. Do you honestly believe you could handle having an eight-year-old boy around all the time?"

"What kind of grandmother will I be if I don't take him in? What will people say if I send my own grandson somewhere else?" We were keeping our voices low because Timmy was in the next room watching "Krypto the Superdog" on the Cartoon Network.

My mother wasn't thinking clearly. It would be impossible for her to take in Timmy—though she was only sixty-seven, in addition to her heart condition, she had arthritic knees that often reduced her to walking with a cane. "Mom," I said, "it's too much for you. He's a sweet boy, and you do fine with him for a day or two. But can you imagine full time? And it wouldn't be just him. There'd be other kids hanging around, too." A loud *boom-boom* drifted into the kitchen from the TV, and my mother cringed. "There'd be a lot of noise like that all the time," I said. "And lots of car pooling. You'd have to get him to swim lessons and baseball practice. Then in the fall, you'd have to get him up for school, help with his homework, go to parent-teacher conferences. Are you up for going through all that again?"

From the living room came the sound of Timmy hitting an imaginary opponent: "Pow pow!" he shouted, and I could hear him moving about, throwing punches.

"I don't know if I could do it," she said, "but I should."

"Look, let's not panic. Uncle Bill didn't say they were never going to take Timmy, just not right away. We can probably come up with a child care plan for the meantime. Maybe Timmy can go to day camp every day, and we'll hire someone to come in and stay with him in his own house the rest of the time. A nanny or something like that. Just until Chris is well enough to go back to college, then Timmy can move to Westerly."

Please let Chris get better soon, please let Uncle Bill and Aunt Millie take Timmy to Westerly. It was almost too much to think about.

"Look," I said, going over to my mother, "we've all had a really hard day. You're beat. Right now, what you need is some quiet time for yourself." And I needed quiet time for myself, too. Time to think. I stood behind her chair and rubbed her shoulders. "Things will work out," I said to her back. But I was afraid that they might not work out at all.

"Mom," I said, "why don't you go into your room and lie down?"

"You want me to sleep? You think I can sleep after all that's happened?"

"Well, then go into the living room and sit in your recliner. Just try to rest a little. You're all worked up."

"Of course, I'm worked up." She twisted a plaid cloth napkin, then used the tip of it to blot her eyes. "My firstborn child was buried today. My only son. I have every reason to be upset."

Leaning down, I pressed my face against her cheek. Her hair smelled like it needed a shampoo. Her body was trembling as I wrapped my arms around her. "Mom, I'm worried about you, that's all." Her tears dropped onto my sleeve, and she wiped her eyes with the soft fabric of my sweater. I whispered into her ear, "Try not to make it worse for Timmy. We need to stay calm for his sake."

None of us slept that night. My mother stretched out in the recliner and dozed off and on, but she never got the healing power of sleep her tired body needed. Timmy didn't put up a fuss when I put him to bed in the room that had been Dan's when he was a boy. A number of Timmy's toys were stuffed under the bed from his regular visits to my mother's house. I searched the box of yellow trucks and plastic police cars until I found the stuffed dog—Pongo the Dalmatian—that he'd dragged around as a toddler. One eye had been lost, which made the dog look as if it were winking, one ear was half torn off, and stuffing spilled out from one of the black dots on the back. Timmy let me put Pongo under his arm, and I pulled the blankets up to his chin. Timmy's eyes were wide open, as if his upper eyelids were taped to his eyebrows. I had a feeling his eyes would stay open all night, even in the dark.

My old bedroom had long ago been changed into a laundry and sewing room, so I went into my mother's bedroom to rest. The quilt on her bed was so worn, it felt like it had a sheen when I lay down on top of it. I pulled an afghan she'd knitted over my feet and dropped my head onto a pillowcase she'd edged with tatting.

I was overtired and unable to fall asleep. I wanted to be home in my own bed. *Soon,* I told myself. *Just hang in there another week. Then you'll be back in your own house.* Of course, that would happen only if we found a solution for Timmy's care.

I could hear my mother out in the living room, snoring lightly, then waking herself with sobbing. It went on like that all night. We were a house of lonely people, each of us separate in our pain. I thought of Timmy in my brother's bed. And for the first time since all this happened, I allowed myself to think of Dan. Poor Danny. He'd never see Timmy grow up. Never see him use that new baseball glove he'd given him. I cried then for my brother and for all that he would be cheated of by dying so young.

I had to talk with Kate, even though it was late. I used my mother's bedside phone, and Kate answered practically on the first ring. I think she'd been waiting for me to call. Kate asked right away about Timmy—she'd remembered the picture he'd drawn that was on the fridge at my cabin.

"I don't really know. I've tried to explain it to him, but I'm not sure how much he understands." I propped myself up in bed, half-sitting against the pillows, my knees drawn up. "Kate, I can't believe how hard all this is." We talked for at least a half hour; she listened patiently while I told her everything that had happened since I'd come back to Providence. Every detail. Even the color of the satin lining in Dan's casket.

Not only did Kate listen to my sorrowful monologue, I could tell that she really cared. "Oh, Sam," she said every so often, "I'm so sorry." Finally, when I was all talked out, she said, "I wish I could be there with you."

"I do too." I knew that somehow all of this would not be quite so difficult if Kate were here.

After I hung up, I lay on my side in my mother's bed, my head on the pillow. The room was hot even with the window open, and sweat pooled behind my knees. I kicked off the afghan and lay uncovered. The noise of the city was a constant din through the screen: traffic driving by on the street, a car alarm going off, neighbors arguing, dogs barking, a tomcat sounding like a human cry. So different from the lilting whippoorwills and peep frogs that sang me to sleep on the mountain. I hugged the extra pillow and curled my body around it, pretending it was Kate. Kate giving me solace and comfort. But a sense of doom kept me awake as I watched the streetlight outside the window throwing shadows from under its steel hat.

Chapter 6

Shell shock. That's all I could think as I drove over the winding blacktop roads to Clayton. I glanced over at Timmy, his little body dwarfed by the Jeep's seat belt. For the entire trip from Providence, his eyes had been wide with bewilderment, a deer-in-the-headlights look. I hoped it was the right thing to bring him back with me to Hurricane Mountain.

When I passed through the intersection of Clayton and the road that curved toward Kate's cottage, I had to hold both hands on the steering wheel to keep the car from turning. There was nothing I wanted more at that moment than to be with Kate, but it was late and Timmy was tired. She and I had talked on the phone every day while I was in Providence, so she knew I was coming home, but not what time. I'd see Kate the next day for sure.

He sat huddled in the corner of the passenger seat. "You warm enough?" I asked, turning on the car's heater. A blast of warm air snaked around our feet. He nodded, but he continued to stare into the dark night, his eyes blankly following the beaming path of the headlights. "Hungry?"

Timmy shook his head, but he hadn't had anything to eat since breakfast, and then he'd just poked at the Lucky Charms floating in his dish of milk.

"Here, take this." I handed him an apple. "Go ahead. Take a bite."

By the light of the dashboard I could see that Timmy gave me a fleeting look, then shyly lowered his eyes. He put the apple to his mouth, his lips pale against the red skin. But he didn't seem to have the energy to bite down, and soon he dropped his hand, bringing the apple to his lap. He twirled it by the stem, then listlessly bounced it from palm to palm.

"Won't be much longer," I assured him. "We're nearly at my cabin." I headed up the mountain through the darkened forest. The headlights caught the image of a fat raccoon waddling across the gravel road and slithering into the undergrowth. I pressed my foot on the brake and stopped, idling the Jeep for a few minutes, waiting. Sure enough, there were her babies—little striped fur balls following their mother across the hazardous road.

I pointed to the tiny creatures, lit up in the yellow beam. "See there, Timmy. Aren't they cute?"

Timmy leaned forward in the seat and peered through the windshield. A parade of tiny raccoons was crossing the road. He gestured with his index finger as he counted. "One, two, three, four." He turned to me, his eyes set deep in his face and serious. "Where's the momma?"

"She's in the bushes there beside the road, waiting for them," I said. "She won't leave her babies."

"Oh," he said in a little voice.

We watched the string of baby raccoons make their way across the road into the ditch, one by one disappearing in the roadside grass. As I shifted into gear, the Jeep lurched slightly and Timmy grabbed his seat belt where it crossed his narrow chest.

At my cabin, the lamp fixtures that hung on each side of the front door had been turned on. Jean must have done that; I'd told her on the phone that we'd be coming in late. I parked, jumped out of the Jeep, and went around to open Timmy's door. It was quite a jump for him to get down, so I held my hands out to catch him. He brushed them away and leaped down by himself.

From the dark pinewoods behind the cabin came the call of a whippoorwill. Usually I liked that birdsong, but that night, it seemed to be the saddest sound I'd ever heard. I grabbed my black suitcase from the back of the Jeep, then reached in for Timmy's red backpack. His large, canvas duffel bag could wait to be unloaded in the morning. Night had settled in, and I was suddenly bone tired.

Looking around, Timmy asked, "Where are all the houses?" In his neighborhood, houses were lined up along both sides of the street.

"Well, my friend Jean's house is over there." His gaze followed my finger to the illumination pooling from a floodlight onto the needles of pine trees.

"How come it's so dark here?" he asked as I handed him a flashlight.

"You're used to street lights," I said. "There aren't any street lights up here on the mountain."

Timmy flicked the flashlight on and off a few times, then shone it around the yard, lighting up the woodpile, the riding lawnmower, the birdfeeder.

"But look up there." I took his chin in my hand and tilted his head. "Look at that sky. Ever see so many stars?"

He leaned his head back. He scanned the overhead sky as he rolled his head from side to side.

"There's the Big Dipper." I held his finger and traced the constellation for him. "That bright star over it is the North Star."

"Where do we sleep?" Timmy asked.

"Oh, in the cabin, of course. Come on, I'll show you." I led him inside. The interior was lit up as well, welcoming us. I tossed Timmy's backpack onto the couch. A week's mail lay in a pile on the kitchen table where Jean had left it. Also, someone had set out two cups with packages of instant hot chocolate. Propped next to one cup was a lavender envelope. I opened it, knowing in my heart who it was from.

Dear Sam,

I'm so sorry for your loss, darling. Please remember that I'm here to talk to, cry with, or just be with when you need a friend.

Love, Kate

I couldn't believe she'd called me *darling* and signed the note *love*. What did she mean by that? Surely, it was just the emotion of the occasion that had prompted her to sign the note with that endearment. Still, I held the lavender paper to my chest and closed my eyes for a moment, envisioning her presence. It seemed forever since I'd seen Kate; the next day couldn't come soon enough.

While Timmy roamed the downstairs, I heated water in the teakettle. When he came back, I motioned for him to sit at the table for his hot chocolate, but he continued standing in the middle of the floor, looking little and lost.

"I'll take this in to your room for you," I said, picking up his cup. "Follow me."

Timmy grabbed his red backpack and followed behind as I showed him the way to the small bedroom I'd been using for storage. In this room, too, I noticed Jean's and Kate's touches. The cardboard cartons of out-of-season clothes, Christmas decorations, and other assorted junk had been shoved along two walls and piled neatly on top of one another. Some yellow Tonka trucks—a bulldozer, a steam shovel, and a dump truck—were lined up on the floor beside the bed. The single bed had been cleared and wore a new spread: blue and red with bold yellow construction trucks printed on it. Lying on the blue pillow was a stuffed dog that looked amazingly like Jean's German shepherd, Badger.

"Go brush your teeth," I said. "The bathroom's just down the hall. You have a toothbrush with you?"

He nodded, holding up his red backpack.

"Okay, go on and get ready for bed." He pattered down the hall. I could hear him in the bathroom, the tiny stream as he emptied his bladder, the faucet running as he brushed his teeth, the sounds of gurgling and spitting. Timmy came back into the bedroom. He had jammed his clothes into his backpack; one leg of his jeans was sticking out from the zipper. He wore a white T-shirt and green plaid boxers. For a moment, I was startled, remembering that my brother always wore boxers. A picture flashed before my eyes of Dan as a teenager, walking around my mother's house in plaid boxers, his legs muscular and hairy. Timmy seemed to be waiting to be told what to do next. "Climb up here," I said, patting the bed. I had pulled the covers down and positioned the stuffed dog between his pillow and the wall so it could keep him company all night. I thought it might be a comfort to have something cuddly next to him.

Timmy climbed onto the bed and wiggled his feet under the

covers. With two hands, he picked up the toy dog by its tail and flung it to the floor. "Where's Pongo?"

I'd forgotten to pack his stuffed Dalmatian. "Pongo stayed with Grandma. Maybe Grandma can mail him to you later."

"I want Pongo now."

"Look, what if we put this new dog here for the night?" I set the toy dog on a large cardboard box next to the bed. The box was labeled *dress clothes* and hadn't been opened since I'd moved to Maine. I handed Timmy the cup of warm cocoa. "If you need anything in the night, I'm just across the hall. Okay?"

Already Timmy had dribbled a little cocoa onto his white T-shirt. But he was sitting up in bed sipping from the cup, and I thought that a good sign.

"Want me to leave the door open?" I asked.

He lifted his mouth from the cup. His lip covered with a frothy mustache, he nodded.

"Good night then," I said, bending down to kiss the top of his head. On the way out, I pulled his door half-closed, letting light from the hallway spill into his room.

I took my own cup of hot chocolate outside and sat on the porch step, listening to peep frogs. I folded my arms across my chest and leaned my head against the screen door. Overhead, the black sky was still dotted with stars. *Star light, star bright* jumped into my mind. I wished my life was back the way it used to be. My life was so much simpler then, less complicated when I had just myself to worry about.

As if anything were as simple as making a wish on a star. As if magic could make Dan and Jennifer come back from the dead. But I wanted that for Timmy's sake and my mother's. I wanted Dan back for my own sake, too. Not just to make my life easier, but because I missed him. His dying left an empty place in my heart that would stay that way as long as I lived.

I missed knowing Dan was in the world, sleeping and walking and carrying the same bag of childhood memories that I had slung over my shoulders. Without him, I felt surprisingly alone. I was the only one now who would remember the kitten we'd rescued from the icy pond behind our house. We'd wrapped it in our mother's quilt—the same quilt that was on her bed to this day—and fed it milk from my doll's bottle. And I was the only one who knew the secret of the Christmas that Dan and I had found gifts in our parents' bedroom closet and opened them all by slitting the tape with a razor blade. After we'd examined each gift, we'd carefully covered the cuts with fresh tape, and our mother never knew we'd spied on Santa. That Christmas morning when we'd *oohed* and *aahed* and acted surprised at Dan's train set and my Barbie house, we'd avoided looking at each other because whenever we caught each other's gaze, we began to giggle. That too would be a solitary memory now to be hoarded by me alone.

Well, Dan was dead. That was the truth of the matter. And Timmy was here, sleeping in the next room. What had I gotten myself into?

The mosquitoes were pestering me, so I stepped back inside the cottage. Timmy's jacket was lying crumpled on the floor where he'd dropped it, and I picked it up and folded it. Suddenly, I dropped my head into the folds of fabric and began to cry, just standing there alone in the room.

I didn't cry for long; the sound of a pickup coming down the lane shook me out of my weeping spell. I assumed it was Jean coming home from the store. Glancing at the clock over the refrigerator, I saw that it was nearly 9:35 p.m., so I figured she'd just go on by to her cabin. But the glow of headlights swept over the kitchen ceiling and I heard her pull into my yard. I peered out the window to see Jean opening her truck door. The cab light flashed on and I saw Badger sitting in the passenger seat, his nose out the half-opened window. Then the cab light went out, and I could hear her knocking softly at the cabin door.

When I let her in, she gave me a hug, which was unusual for Jean. It was just a dart in with open arms, then jump back out again. But still it was a hug, quick as it was. "You hanging in there?" she asked gruffly, stepping over to the fridge and helping herself to a can of Miller Lite. She held the can up for me in the way of asking if I'd like one, too.

"Pepsi's fine," I said. "The caffeine-free one."

Setting the two cans on the table, she pulled out a chair and sat down. "Rough week, huh?" she asked, sliding the Pepsi toward me.

"You don't know the half of it." I dropped into the chair across the table from her.

She snapped open her can and took a swig of beer. "Where's the boy?"

I pointed to the back bedroom. "Sleeping. He's worn out." I opened my can of soda but just ran my finger around the rim instead of drinking it. "By the way, thanks for keeping an eye on things here while I was gone."

"It wasn't just me. Kate bought the bedspread for Timmy's room. She picked up the Tonka trucks for him. I guess she has lots of brothers and sisters, so she knows what kids like better than I do."

"I really appreciate all that you both did. I'll see Kate tomorrow and tell her that in person. I bet you're responsible for the stuffed dog, though, right?"

"Hey, I couldn't pass it up. It could be Badger's puppy." Jean chuckled.

Her comment made me smile. "The resemblance is certainly there." I didn't tell her that Timmy had thrown the toy dog onto the floor and refused to keep it in his bed.

Jean stretched her legs and placed her feet in the empty chair between us. "So tell me about Providence." I knew that meant she was here to listen, and it didn't take much for me to let it all out. She sipped her beer and listened while I told her how I'd cleaned Dan's house and how hard it had been on my mother to see his things boxed up.

"You put it up for sale?"

"Had to. There's no way my mother or I could afford to keep it. There wasn't any insurance on the mortgage. Dan and Jennifer did leave a life insurance policy for Timmy, but it was just a small one." I took a sip of Pepsi. "I mean, who really believes they're going to die young like that? Dan was just thirty-eight. Jennifer was thirty-seven. Think about it—that's close to our ages, you and me, Jean. When you're under forty, you think you've got time before you have to worry about stuff like life insurance."

49

Jean folded back the hem of a pants leg and scratched her shin. I could see that she was sticking to her vow of never shaving her legs. "How long will you be keeping Timmy?"

"That's a question I can't answer. My aunt and uncle were planning to take him shortly after the funeral, but they bowed out at the last minute. My cousin got sick." I rose from the table to find something for us to snack on. "My mother's not up to it," I said over my shoulder, rummaging through the cupboard for peanuts or crackers or pretzels. "She had that heart spell last winter, you know. I'm Dan's only sibling. And Jennifer was an only child, so no help there."

"Get me another beer while you're up, will you?" Jean tossed her empty can into the recycling bin next to the front door. "What about your sister-in-law's folks? Couldn't Timmy live with them?"

I handed her another cold beer and set a box of Triscuits on the table. "Her parents are quite a bit older. I guess Jennifer was a change-of-life baby. Totally unexpected, from what she told me." I sat down. "Her mother and father couldn't even make it to the funeral. Several years ago, they moved from Rhode Island to Arizona into a retirement community. Timmy was just a baby when they left, probably doesn't even remember them. Jennifer's dad is big on golfing, and their condo is right on the edge of the ninth hole. But her mother has failed a lot lately, at least that's what my mother told me. In fact, I think she's living in some kind of nursing home near the condo."

"Well, if Jennifer's parents aren't in any position to take Timmy, there's always the state system. Have you thought of that? He could live with a foster family." Jean raised an eyebrow at me as she said this.

"You know what I'm going to say to that. No way." Opening the box of crackers, I offered her some. "Somebody in our family has to give Timmy a home. He has to be with real family."

Jean thrust her hand into the box and came out with a fistful of salty crackers. "Doesn't sound like there's much family to choose from."

"I haven't given up totally on my aunt and uncle yet." I tilted one cracker on its edge, playing with it, twirling it. "So to get back to your original question, I don't know for sure how long Timmy will be here with me, but it's just until I find someone else to take him."

"It'll be different having a kid on the mountain," Jean said with her mouth full. She swallowed, then added, "You'll have to keep a close eye on him during hunting season."

I dropped the cracker I was playing with onto the table, and it snapped in half. "Come on!" Of course, Jean knew I hated hunting; what she didn't know was that I hated the idea that Timmy might still be with me in the fall. "That's months away! He won't even be here then."

"You can't count on that," Jean said, and I was mad at her for putting words to my thoughts.

As Jean was leaving, I remembered to ask her how things were at the store.

"Busy. Crazy." She dropped her second beer can into the recycling bin. "You know, the usual for this time of year. Crawling with tourists. But that's okay because they all have money in their pockets." Jean went out the door, and Badger let out a bark to greet her. I waved as she backed out and turned toward her cedar house farther down the lane.

What struck me now was the silence. I was alone for the first time in over a week. Timmy was in the other room, sleeping, but there wasn't any noise except the humming of the refrigerator and the ticking of the kitchen clock. Quiet. How I loved it, craved it. Suddenly, I needed to be in my studio, needed to be with my painting things. I hung Timmy's jacket in the closet and climbed the stairs to the loft, hitting the electrical switch on my way up. The upstairs lights came on, illuminating my studio.

Yes, this was my world, this was where I belonged. Everything was just as I'd left it. There was my worktable with its wonderful clutter. I leaned against the table's edge and ran my fingertips over brushes in a coffee can. My easel stood beside the window with the unfinished hummingbird painting. There was a line of dust on the top of the canvas, and I wiped it off.

I stood back from the easel and studied the painting, seeing what needed to be done to finish it. Would I ever get back to this work, ever find the quiet time to come up here and paint in the morning light? This is what I would not give up.

But what would I do with Timmy while I worked?

Chapter 7

Surprisingly, I was able to work on my painting the next morning. I woke early after having slept in my own bed to the sounds of birds chattering, a music I'd missed while I was in the city. Folding back the patchwork quilt, I sat up and admired the log walls varnished with age, the pewter lamp on my bedside table, a rag rug warming the pine board floor, plaid curtains blowing in the morning breeze. Such a lovely little refuge.

Waiting above me in the loft was my real sanctuary: my studio. I threw on some clothes and went to check on Timmy. He was still sleeping, all tangled up in his sheets, the new construction bedspread in a lump by his feet. I took advantage of the time before he woke and eagerly climbed the stairs to my studio. The unfinished canvas was bathed in early morning sun. I got to work, quickly falling into the rhythm of painting. Several hours must have passed while I worked.

"Aunt Sam?"

Lost in my work, I'd nearly forgotten about Timmy. He stood at the top of the stairs, wearing the plaid boxers and white T-shirt he'd worn to bed. His blond hair was mussed from sleep, and he was carrying the stuffed dog by one ear.

"Oh, hi, Timmy. I'll be with you in just a minute." I mixed indigo blue to the yellow paint on my palette until I got the green hue I wanted for the hummingbird's feathers. Soon, I was engaged again with the painting, adding more blue to deepen the shadows.

"I didn't have breakfast yet," Timmy said.

"Well, you're on a new diet," I joked as I brushed paint onto the canvas. "How's one meal a day sound?"

"What do you mean?"

I glanced over at him and saw a dumbfounded look on his face. "Just a joke, Timmy."

"Oh. My mom always fixes me breakfast when I get up."

"Can't you get it yourself? Make some toast and pour a glass of orange juice?"

He banged the stuffed dog against his leg. "My mom does that for me."

I could see it was a losing battle. "Okay, okay." I cleaned the brush and wiped the bristles with a paint-stained cloth. "I'll make some breakfast. I think I can find a few eggs to fry."

"I don't like eggs. My mom doesn't make me eat them."

I set the brush bristle end up in the can on the worktable. "I'm sure we'll find something."

"How about Cap'n Crunch? I like that. Or Froot Loops."

"The only cereal I have is oatmeal. Do you like that, with brown sugar and raisins?"

He made a face. "I don't think so."

"Well, go on down, and I'll be there in a minute."

He pattered in his bare feet down the open staircase. Feeling frustrated at being torn away from my work, I followed him down to the kitchen.

He was already sitting at the table, and the toy dog was lying on the floor near his chair. I set a small plate and a paper napkin in front of him. Jean had laid in a few groceries from the store, so I had milk and bread and a few other essentials. "Guess it will have to be toast, after all," I said, popping two slices of whole wheat bread into the toaster. "Do you want peanut butter or honey on it?"

"Grape jelly," he said as he carefully watched my every move.

"I don't have any jelly." I peered into the fridge and found a jar of apple butter. "We'll use this."

"I don't like that." He kicked the toy dog with his toe.

"Have you ever tried it?"

"No, but I know I don't like it. At my house, we have grape jelly."

I tried to keep my voice gentle. "Timmy, I have honey or apple butter or peanut butter. That's it. You choose."

"Butter."

I was thinking of my work waiting for me upstairs in the loft. "Do you mean apple butter or peanut butter?"

"Just butter. The yellow kind in a stick."

His toast popped, and I spread farmer's butter on it. When I placed the two slices on his plate, he asked, "Where's the bacon?"

"We don't have any." I poured him a glass of orange juice. "I never eat meat, so there's no bacon in the house."

"Not ever?" He took a sip of juice.

"What?" I said halfheartedly as I leaned over the stove and lit the gas under the teakettle.

"You really don't ever eat meat? Not even McDonald's cheeseburgers?" His mouth was full of toast, his lips smeared with butter.

I reached for a cup in the cupboard and dropped a tea bag into it. "No, I'm a vegetarian."

"Oh. We're Methodists, my mom and dad and me."

I had to chuckle. "Are you finished?" I asked when his plate was empty except for a few golden crumbs.

"I didn't get any bacon." He set his empty juice glass on the table with a thud.

"Timmy, I just explained that to you. There isn't any bacon."

His eyes filled with tears. "When I get back home, I'm going to have all the bacon my mom lets me eat. My dad likes it, too, and sometimes we both eat four slices."

Good god, didn't he understand at all? He was never going home; some other family was going to buy that house. His mother and father were dead. He would not see them again. Never sit at the breakfast table with them, having a contest with Dan to see who could eat the most bacon.

I decided maybe I was being too harsh with him, so I softened my voice. "Look out that window behind you." Timmy swiveled in his chair. "See that tiny bird near the feeder? The red sugar water attracts him. I'm painting a picture of a hummingbird like that."

"Red's my favorite color," Timmy said as he leaned his palms on the window.

This was the first positive thing he'd offered all morning. "Like that sunset we saw last night when we were driving through New Hampshire?" On our drive here from Providence, we'd watched the sun going down behind the White Mountains, and it was a spectacular swirl of reds and oranges. Timmy hadn't commented on it then.

"Um-hum." He pressed his face closer to the window and blew, watching the wispy marks his breath made on the glass.

"Hummingbirds love red, so lots of times you'll see them hovering near the feeder," I said. "Watch how fast his wings are going. That's how he can stay in one place like that."

"Oh," Timmy said, turning away from the window. "What's the big deal? Where I live, we got helicopters flying in the sky, and they can stay in one place, too."

The hummingbird, which I could watch all day, had held his attention for less than two minutes. It could turn out to be boring around here for a city boy.

While Timmy was washing up and brushing his teeth in the bathroom, I phoned Kate. The joy in her voice when she realized it was me made my heart skip.

"Are you really home?"

"Yes, and I miss you," I said. "When can I see you?"

"Soon," she promised.

I felt better just talking with Kate. When Timmy came back into the kitchen, he had such a hangdog look that I decided to try to cheer him up. We took his new trucks outside for him to play in the sandy driveway. I carried the dump truck and bulldozer, one in each hand, and he carried the steam shovel with both hands.

"You can have your own construction site here." I set the trucks down.

"Who do I play with?" he asked, looking around at the vast expanse of meadow and forest and mountains.

"I'll play with you for a little while." I picked up a few stones from the driveway and dropped them into the bed of the dump truck. They made a clunk as they hit the yellow metal. "But then I have a lot of work to do, so you'll have to play by yourself."

"Where's the other kids?"

Digging up sand with my hands, I added that to the stones in the dump truck. "What kids do you mean?"

He was still holding the steam shovel out in front of him with both hands, like it was a hot potato. "Neighbors and stuff."

I lowered the blade on the toy bulldozer and scraped gravel into a small hill. "Well, you can see there aren't any neighbors close by. And I don't often see any kids around here, except sometimes at Bernice's. Her grandchildren, I guess."

"Who's Bernice?"

"A neighbor," I said. "She's got a cabin across the road, but you can't see her place from here."

"That's not a real neighbor. At my house, I got Matt and Justin, they live next to each other just down the street, and if you go through my backyard, there's LaMont and Darnell, they're brothers."

"I know there are a lot of kids near your house. But for now, we're here on the mountain, and there just aren't any around."

"Let's go to the park then."

"Timmy, there isn't any park. We're not in the city with playgrounds and parks. You have to make your own fun." I took the steam shovel from him. "Look, we can pick up this sand and dump it into the truck. Just like real construction guys." I maneuvered the steam shovel and scooped up the pile of sand and stones. Nodding to him, I said, "Go ahead, dump it into the back of the truck."

Timmy sat down in the middle of the driveway and made a halfhearted attempt to raise the scoop. Much of the sand trickled out before it reached its destination, but he managed to move the arm over the truck and open the shovel.

"Isn't that fun?" I asked as the load emptied into the truck. "Where do you want to move the dirt? Do we want to build a road with it?"

He shrugged.

"Push the truck to where you want to build a new road," I

said, placing his hand on the cab. He didn't make any effort, so I pressed his hand and the truck moved ahead a few feet. "Shall we dump it here?"

"Okay," he said, but he didn't make any move to turn the crank and lift the truck bed.

I did it for him, and he watched blankly as the sand and stones sifted into a new pile.

The phone rang inside the cabin. "You stay here and play while I get that," I said, dashing toward the door. It was my mother checking to see that we had made the trip safely from Providence. "We're all settled in," I said. "Timmy slept late this morning, and now we were just outside playing with Tonka trucks." She asked if she could talk to him. "Just a minute, Mom." I covered the mouthpiece with my hand and called out the door for Timmy to come to the phone.

I busied myself fixing a cup of tea, but I could hear his side of the conversation. First, he told her what he had for breakfast—and especially what he didn't have for breakfast. Then he said how everything was different from Providence. "Aunt Sam's is the only house, and there's no sidewalks or streetlights. It's really dark here at nighttime. I was scared." There was a pause while my mother said something. "And, Grandma? I don't have anyone to play with. We're way out in the woods, and there aren't even any other kids." He threw a quick glance in my direction, then turned his back to me and whispered into the phone, "I don't like it here."

I was leaning against the counter, drinking the tea. That's all my mother needs to hear, I thought, how miserable Timmy is. As if she didn't have enough grief of her own. I nudged his shoulder. "Why don't you finish up now and say goodbye?"

He nodded, but kept on talking into the phone. "Grandma, I'm going to see if Aunt Sam will take me to the mall today and get me some Matchbox cars. Maybe we can stop at McDonald's and I can get a Happy Meal. Aunt Sam doesn't eat hamburger, did you know that? I thought everybody in the whole world liked hamburgers and cheeseburgers. All my friends do. I wonder what Aunt Sam will get at McDonald's."

I couldn't imagine what my mother said to that. She knew there wasn't a fast-food place anywhere near Hurricane Mountain. The nearest one was in Fredericksville, and the closest store of any size—Wal-Mart—was there, too.

Timmy said, "I miss you too, Grandma," and handed me the phone.

My mother sounded tired. "Have you been getting any sleep at all?" I asked her. As I listened to her litany of insomnia, I picked up Timmy's new toy dog from the floor and handed it to him. He shook his head, refusing to take it. "Go back outside," I mouthed to him, and he ran out of the kitchen.

"Look, Mom, maybe you need to see the doctor," I said, then listened while she gave me excuses. "You won't be bothering the doctor. That's what she gets paid for. Just call and see if she has an opening." I set down my cup with its spent tea bag. "If you're not resting better in a few days, you should call her. You can't keep going without sleep." My mother's health and her state of mind worried me. I was afraid she might never recover from the loss of her son.

"Don't go worrying about me. I'm going to be fine."

I didn't believe her. She asked how I thought Timmy was adjusting, and I used that word, too: *fine*. We were trying to protect each other. Outside the window, a hummingbird had flown in and was fighting with another one over the red feeder. They dove at each other, retreated, dove again. "Mom, have you talked with Uncle Bill recently? How's Christina?" What I really wanted to know was when she'd be well enough for Uncle Bill to take Timmy. My heart sank when my mother told me that my cousin was still in the hospital and that her recuperation was slow. "So it's going to be a while before Uncle Bill and Aunt Millie know if they'll go ahead with their original plan?" My mother said yes, it seemed that way. "Let me know as soon as you hear anything, okay?"

There would be some major changes in my life if Timmy ended up staying with me for the summer. What did I know about raising a kid? I couldn't even fix him a proper breakfast.

We managed to get through the day. I kept Timmy busy helping me stack wood beside the shed. "Is this how it goes?" he asked, dropping a piece of wood onto the pile.

"Yes, but we need to keep it neat. Like this." I showed him how to stack the wood so that it would stay in a neat pile.

He worked hard, carrying split logs one by one to the woodpile. But I had to rearrange nearly every log he set down. The job would have gone much more quickly if I were doing it myself. Having a kid around was already wearing me out.

In the cabin, I pointed him toward the pine bookcase in the living room, hoping he might find something there to keep him entertained while I got caught up on some chores. The shelves held art history books, texts on process, old issues of *Art in America*, books showing the work of female artists: Cassatt, Kahlo, Krasner, Morisot. I hoped Timmy would enjoy looking at the pictures and left him on his knees thumbing though a book of O'Keeffe's desert paintings. I settled in at the kitchen table to write to my agent, Riley, explaining why I'd be late with the hummingbird painting for the gallery in New Hampshire. I just hoped I'd find time to finish the project so the painting could hang in the exhibit.

Fifteen minutes hadn't passed when Timmy stood behind me and said, "Aunt Sam, it's time for 'Rocket Power.'"

"I don't know what that is." I licked a stamp and placed it in the corner of the envelope, then addressed it to Riley.

"You know. 'Rocket Power'" Timmy acted as if I were really dumb, as if it were something everyone in the world knew. "It's a TV show about this boy named Otto Rocket. His sister's name is Reggie. And he's got these friends, Twister and Sam. Only this Sam is a boy, not a girl like you. They do all kinds of extreme sports, like skateboarding and other stuff like that."

It was beginning to dawn on me. "Is this a cartoon you're talking about?"

"Yeah. It comes on every day at 3:30. When I get home from school, I get to watch it and have a snack." He scanned the kitchen and living room. "Where's the TV?"

As if it should be standard furniture. "I don't have a television set."

I could see that now I'd really gone beyond all reason in his estimation. He stomped his foot as if he couldn't believe what he'd heard. "Everybody's got a TV. In my house, we got three. One in the living room, a great big one downstairs in the family room, one in my Mom and Dad's bedroom. And when I get older, like maybe fifth grade, I'm going to have a TV in my bedroom."

"Well, I don't own a single television."

"How am I going to watch 'Hey Arnold'? Or 'Jimmy Neutron'? This is the dumbest place I've ever been at. Why can't I go to Grandma's? She's got a TV and a VCR and a DVD. She gets movies at Blockbuster, and we saw 'Finding Nemo' and 'Monster's, Inc.' And I bet we watched 'A Bug's Life' at least ten times. Me and Grandma like that the best."

"You can't go to Grandma's because she's not feeling well."

"What's wrong with her?"

"She feels tired and her heart is giving her trouble."

"She's not going to die, is she?"

"No, of course not. She'll be fine. She just needs to rest."

I threw together a supper of potato salad on a bed of lettuce. He picked out all the pieces of hard-boiled egg and pushed them to the side of his plate, whining about not having steak like his dad cooked on the grill. When we finished supper, Timmy again wanted to watch TV; he couldn't imagine life without it. I entertained him by devising a game of Pick Up Sticks with colored toothpicks I found in the cupboard.

Just before dark, Kate showed up. I was so glad to see her. How lovely she was: tall willowy body, short dark hair, warm gray eyes. She gave me a long hug, and it felt so good to be in her arms. Softly, she said into my ear, "I'm sorry about your brother." Then she held me at arm's length and looked at me closely. "Are you doing okay?"

I felt a lump in my throat. "I'm not sure." I gave her a weak grin. "Thanks for the trucks. That was very generous. As you can imagine, I don't have much here in the way of toys."

Kate smiled. "Well, are you going to introduce me to the guy who drives those trucks?"

Timmy was sitting on the floor in front of the fireplace, leaning colored toothpicks into the shape of a tent. I said, "This is the woman who gave you those nice Tonka trucks."

"Hi there, Timmy." Reaching down, she shook his hand. "I'm glad to meet you. My name's Kate." She got right down on the floor with him. "What do you have here?"

"Pick Up Sticks, but they're not real. Aunt Sam just has these dumb toothpicks."

"Looks to me like they might work just fine. Here, let's try them. You show me how." He showed her how to pick up the sticks, and he laughed when Kate dropped hers. "Maybe this doesn't work so well, after all," she said, laughing along with him. "I have another idea. How about a game of Monopoly?"

He brightened up at that. "Yeah. Me and Grandma play that. I like to have the car, and she always takes the wheelbarrow."

Kate went out to her Ford to get the cardboard box, and I poured us each a glass of lemonade. We sat around the kitchen table for an hour and a half, buying and selling houses. Of course, we let Timmy win. He moved his little silver car with great earnestness around the board and hoarded his pile of fake money. Kate set the board game on a shelf in the living room. "I'll leave it here in case we want to play again sometime, okay, Timmy?"

We all moved outside and sat on the front step. Kate suggested we count fireflies. "Oh, there's just too many." she exclaimed when we reached forty-nine. "We'll never count them all."

"Fifty," Timmy said, pointing to a small blinking light. "Right there. That makes fifty."

"And there's at least another fifty over there in the field," I said. "Kate's right. Too many to count. Besides, it's your bedtime."

"I don't want to go to bed. I want to stay here and look at the fireflies."

"You can see them from your bedroom window. Say good night to Kate now and go get ready for bed."

Timmy scowled and mumbled, "Night," as he got up from the step and headed inside the cabin.

"Good night, Timmy," Kate said, reaching out and patting his arm as he passed her. "Maybe next time we can catch some of those fireflies, and you can put some in a jar to make a light for your room."

"Would that work? I mean, would they really light up inside the house?"

"Sure, when it's dark. You'll need to make a habitat for them. Put some grass in the jar to make them feel at home. And you'll need to punch some holes in the cover so they get air. Then after a day or two, you can let them go."

"Would I have to?"

I said, "They'll die if you keep them in the jar. You don't want that to happen, do you?" Timmy looked at me with wide eyes, and I knew I'd made a blunder. I glanced helplessly at Kate, but she nodded, letting me know it was okay to mention death.

"I don't like it when things die," Timmy said.

"None of us do, Timmy," Kate reassured him. "It's always very sad when something dies. I bet you feel sad about your mommy and daddy, right?"

"I wasn't talking about that," Timmy said. "I was just talking about fireflies."

"Well, like I said, we'll catch some of those fireflies one of these nights. Okay?"

He nodded as he stared at the ground. He turned and walked into the cabin, his shoulders slumped.

"Poor little guy," Kate said when he was out of earshot. "What a lot for him to process. How's he dealing with it all?"

"I'm not sure. I don't think he's cried, and that seems strange to me."

"It's not real to him yet. He's probably still in shock. He'll cry when it hits him that his parents are really gone."

"I appreciate your help with him," I said. "I feel at a loss. I haven't had much experience with kids. Half the time, I don't know what to say to him. This is kind of like the blind leading the blind here."

"I've had a lot of experience with my brothers and sisters. As the oldest of six, I practically raised the last two after my mother went to work." Kate squeezed my hand. "The best thing is to just be natural. It'll all fall into place."

"If I don't fall on my face first," I said. "I'm going to go tuck him into bed. That much about mothering I do know."

"See? It comes to you naturally." Kate laughed.

When I came back, I pulled the screen door quietly closed behind me and joined Kate on the front step. "He was nearly asleep already. I tried to give him a kiss on the cheek, but he wouldn't let me."

"Give him time. It's best not to push him." She stretched her arms over her head. "Mmm, it's so peaceful here."

"Follow me," I said, taking her hand and leading her to the lawn in front of the cabin. I sat on the grass and pulled her down beside me. "Look up." I pointed to the sky. "Isn't that amazing?"

She lay back and sighed. "Incredible. It's almost too much to take in."

For a while, we watched the sweep of sky pinpointed with dots of light. Kate broke the silence. "To think, they're there all the time. All those stars."

"Yeah, we just can't see them until we get away from man-made light."

"I think most of the time," she said, "we just don't pay attention. We don't bother to see what's in front of us."

I wasn't surprised when Kate held her arms out to me. I fell into her comforting embrace there on the grass, and we began kissing: a delicious tangle of lips and mouths and tongues.

Chapter 8

In the morning, Timmy was still sleeping, so I thought it was safe to step outside for a moment of quiet before he woke. I dressed in shorts and a sleeveless shirt, then carried my cup of tea outside and let the serenity of the morning fill me up. Hurricane Mountain was the picture of peace. The sky's rich blue tapestry was threaded with wispy clouds that hung over the neighboring mountains. I took a deep breath and drank in the air, sweet with the smell of unmowed grass. Cardinals whistled from high in pine trees, and orioles picked at the flesh of an orange half I'd nailed to the gnarled apple tree.

I wandered along the path behind my cottage until I came to a stream, and I followed along the bank to a spot where the stream widened into a deep pool. I paused and was looking into the pool when I heard a branch snapping behind me. Timmy stood on the footpath, wearing the T-shirt he'd worn to bed. He'd pulled on a pair of jeans, but his boxers were sticking out over the waistband. He wasn't wearing socks, and his sneakers were unlaced. "Good morning," I said. "I thought you were sleeping."

"I got scared." He gave me a quick glance, then kicked at dead leaves with the toe of his sneaker. "I woke up and you were gone. I was all alone."

"How did you find me?"

"I followed the path."

"I wasn't far away, was I?"

The way he glared at me, you would have thought I'd been a hundred miles away, not just a hundred feet down the path.

"Come here," I said. "Closer." He shuffled over to where I stood at the bank of the stream. I lightly tousled his hair with my hand; his head was damp with sweat where he'd been sleeping on it. "What would you think of a swim?"

"Here?" He looked up and down the stream. "Is it deep enough?"

"It is where it widens out. See? By that big boulder." I pointed to a huge rock jutting out of the middle of the stream. "There's a nice deep pool there. We can't really swim much, but it's great for cooling off. And it's better than taking a bath."

"Oh," he said, without enthusiasm.

"When we want a real swim, we'll go down to the state park on Lake Rand. But just for a quick dip, this is perfect. Trust me." I picked up a stone and tossed it into the pool of clear water. It plunked as it hit the surface, then sank. "Let's try it."

"Don't we need bathing suits?"

"No, just take off your sneakers and jeans." I untied my Reeboks and kicked them off my feet. Leaning my hand on Timmy's shoulder for support, I stuck my foot into the stream. "Mmm," I murmured.

"Is it cold?" he asked, wiggling out from under my hand.

"Like ice," I smiled. "Coming in?"

"Nah. I'll just watch."

"It's up to you." Still wearing my shorts and sleeveless shirt, I stepped into the stream. Timmy waited on the bank, his hands shoved into the back pockets of his jeans. He was oblivious to the fact that he'd forgotten to zip his fly.

"Change your mind?" I asked, as I waded deeper. He shook his head. Spreading my arms, I let the water lift me until I was floating on my back. The sun was bright, and patches of blue sky pierced through green leaves. A pair of swallows flew over the water. Savoring the refreshing chill of the stream, I closed my eyes. Maybe Timmy would decide to venture in if I ignored him. After a while, I opened my eyes and rolled my head to look at him. He was still standing in the same spot, hands in his back pockets, watching me.

It didn't look like my ploy was going to work, so I kicked my feet down until I found the stony bottom. When I stood, the water was waist deep. I walked over to the edge of the stream and scrambled up the grassy bank. Shaking my head like a dog, I sprinkled Timmy with drops of water. "I'm gonna get you wet one way or another." I laughed. I was hoping to get a smile out of him, but he scowled and jumped back. "Maybe we should go back to the cabin. Is that what you want?"

"I don't care."

I slipped my damp feet into my Reeboks and headed up the path. Behind me came the soft crunch of feet as Timmy followed.

To assuage Timmy's disappointment—I guess you could call it outright disbelief—that there weren't any malls or fast-food places for miles around, I opted to take him to Jean's Village Store. He seemed to like riding in the Jeep, and I took the top off, which he really enjoyed. When we came to the intersection of our lane and the gravel road, he noticed Bernice's place across the way. "Who lives there?"

"Remember I told you that I have a neighbor named Bernice? That's where she stays when she comes up on the mountain to fish or hunt."

"Is Bernice the one you said who has kids around sometimes?"

"Sometimes. I've seen a couple of boys there once in a while."

"How old are they?"

"Oh, I don't know. I've never really paid any attention. Close to your age, I guess."

"Maybe they'll be around sometime, and I can play with them."

I didn't think that was going to happen, but I said, "We'll see."

In fifteen minutes, we came into Clayton, and as usual for this time of year, the tiny parking lot in front of Jean's store was jammed with dust-covered Jeeps, SUVs, and vans. I waited at the edge of the road while a group of kids dressed in bathing suits and sucking on taffy sticks piled into a Dodge Caravan. When the van backed out, I pulled in next to Jean's red pickup. Timmy smiled widely when he saw her German shepherd sleeping in the back on a pile of blankets. "Timmy," I said as I shut off the engine, "there's a bag of doggie treats in the glove compartment. Why don't you get those out for Badger?"

"Is that his name?" he asked as he fumbled with the latch.

I leaned over and helped him flip open the glove compartment. "Yes. That's Jean's dog. He's very friendly." I stepped out of the Jeep. "Bring him a treat."

Timmy jumped down from the Jeep with the plastic baggy in his hand. He wasn't shy at all when he approached the truck. "Hey, there, Badger," he crooned. "You're a good boy."

The dog jumped to his feet, placed his front paws on the edge of the truck bed, and wagged his tail frantically. Timmy climbed onto the tailgate so he could pet him. "What do you want, huh?" Timmy said, rubbing his neck. "Think I've got something for you?" Timmy slipped him a doggie bone. Badger took hold of it with his teeth, tossed his head as he chomped on it, and with an abundance of saliva running out the corners of his mouth, he swallowed the treat.

Jean was coming out the screen door, her arms full of paper bags. "Samantha Warren, are you teaching that boy to give Badger treats? That dog's going to be big as a moose." She laughed.

"Hello to you, too," I said. Jean handed me the grocery bags before she opened the back door of a dusty Saab that had a canoe strapped to its roof. Taking the bags from me, she set them on the seat just as a customer came out of the store carrying a six-pack of Canada Dry ginger ale in each hand. "You're all set there," she told the man as she closed his back door. "Enjoy your stay in Clayton. If you need anything, we're open all summer, from dawn to dusk. Weekends included." He nodded at her across the roof of the car, then slid the soda pop onto the front seat and climbed in. As he backed out of the tiny parking lot, I observed the Connecticut plate on his car. Many of the tourists came from the New England states and New York. "Have a good day now," Jean called.

Jean never seemed to tire of being pleasant to the customers, asking the locals about their families or giving advice to the tourists about where to stay in the Clayton area. But nobody would accuse Jean McCray of being *Miss Nice*. You wouldn't want to cross her. She could be downright mean if the occasion called for it. Once, right in the middle aisle of the store, she kneed a drunken customer who'd reached out to grope her ample breasts. Nobody ran roughshod over Jean McCray, which was probably why she was able to make a go of it in this rough-and-tumble rural area.

She turned to us. "You must be Timmy," she said to him. "I see you've made friends with Badger already." Reaching into the truck bed, she lifted out a red bowl. She dumped water onto the sandy parking lot, then handed the empty bowl to Timmy. "Here, you can be in charge of filling this up with fresh water. There's a faucet in the store."

Timmy nodded and took the bowl, but his shyness had returned. We followed Jean up the wooden steps into the store, and I noticed how the fabric of her plaid cotton shirt stretched across her broad back. A well-thumbed map of the local hiking trails stuck out of the back pocket of her jeans.

Inside the store, a brown ceramic cup with my initials—*SW*— hung on a hook over the unlit potbelly woodstove. I filled my cup with coffee from the ever-present pot and sat in a wooden rocker near the bay window. The window ledge was strewn with newspapers and magazines. I thumbed through a copy of the *Fredericksville Journal* while Timmy roamed around the store, inspecting the shelves of candy, the displays of fishing lures, the dusty boxes of cereal, the stacked cans of soup. I let him buy some SweeTarts and a bottle of Gatorade, and Jean made a fresh Italian sandwich for him and one without ham or salami for me.

In the parking lot, Timmy stopped by Jean's truck to give Badger his bowl of fresh water. In exchange, Timmy got a face full of lapping tongue, which made him giggle. Badger gave two short barks. "He's saying goodbye," Timmy said, waving at the dog. Badger thumped his tail and settled back into the pile of blankets. "Will we see him again?"

"Badger? Of course. Jean lives near me, remember? You'll get to see Badger lots this summer."

He bit into a SweeTart. "Not when I go home."

"Let's walk over to the flea market," I said to take his mind off any thought of going back to Providence anytime soon. The flea market was set up in a U-shape in front of Town Hall, and a string of wooden tables displayed assorted stuff for sale: antique hand tools, used fishing lures, old baseball cards, Christmas ornaments, military paraphernalia, LP collections, carnival glass, overpriced school lunch boxes from the fifties and sixties, old hunting knives, huge silver belt buckles etched with deer or bear, fliers advertising taxidermists. Timmy was delighted to find a table littered with used toys.

We carried a carton full of Matchbox cars and buildings back to the Jeep. In the parking lot, Timmy stopped to say another goodbye to Badger. I was setting the box in the backseat when I looked up to see Garret Belling going up the steps of The Village Store. I turned my back so he wouldn't spot me, and as soon as he went inside the store, I jumped into the Jeep and started the motor. "We're leaving," I called to Timmy. He patted Badger on the head one more time. "Right now," I hissed. Timmy climbed into the passenger side, and I tore out of the parking lot before Garret re-emerged from the store.

I drove on through the village intersection in the direction of Hurricane Mountain. As I passed the turnoff to Kate's cottage, I wondered if she was there or if she'd gone into Fredericksville to work on campus. I wanted to stop, but I was riled up from seeing Garret and I was afraid I'd do nothing but complain and blow off steam. I didn't want to keep unloading my problems onto Kate. Instead, I wanted to remember her kisses the night we lay on the grass at my cabin.

On our way up the mountain, I crossed a wooden bridge over a brook. Just beyond the bridge, something was suspended low in a tree and hung out over the road. "What's that?" Timmy asked.

"I don't know. Let's investigate." I shut off the motor, and we jumped down from the Jeep. When we walked closer to the object in the tree, I gasped.

"What is it, Aunt Sam?" Timmy asked. "It looks like a bare-naked cat."

We were looking at a raccoon that had been gutted and skinned. It was hanging with rope twined around each hind leg.

Along the exposed muscles of the carcass, stringy tendons caught the sun's rays through the leaves and glistened. The front paws hung down like helpless hands, and tied to one paw was a piece of orange paper.

"Is it a cat?" Timmy asked. "Why's it look like that?"

"No." I could hear the tremble in my voice. "It's a raccoon. Somebody has been very mean to hurt it like that."

I moved closer to the coon to examine the piece of paper. When I discovered it was from one of my *No Hunting* signs, I jumped back. Was this meant as another spiteful message for me?

"Aunt Sam, is it the same raccoon we saw crossing the road? What's going to happen to her babies? We've got to find them and help them," he said as he started toward the ditch.

I wanted to get out of there in case whoever had done this was still around, watching us from the woods. "We're going back to the cabin right now," I said, catching Timmy by his shirttail. "We'll never find small animals in that tall grass. Besides, it's probably not even the same raccoon."

"I think it's the mother raccoon!" His face looked like he wanted to cry, but he held it in, his body heaving with the effort to hold back tears. "What will the babies do without their mom? What's going to happen to them?"

Leaning against the Jeep, I pulled him to me and tried to comfort him as I watched the woods carefully for any sign of human motion.

In the days following our encounter with the dead raccoon, Timmy became quiet; he seemed to pull into himself even more. In one corner of the cabin's living room, he'd constructed a village of houses and roads with the Matchbox cars and buildings. He played for hours in this imaginary world: miniature fire station, police station, library, post office, a school with tiny yellow school buses, and a house that opened to reveal plastic people living their perfect lives.

Watching him play, I glimpsed my chance to escape to the work waiting for me in the loft studio. "I'm going upstairs,

Timmy," I said. "You just stay here and play. Try to be quiet." I made a gesture of zipping my mouth with my finger and thumb. "Very, very quiet so I can work."

He nodded as he drove the yellow bus up to the schoolhouse. "Aunt Sam, is it okay if I go like this—*vroom, vroom?*" he said, making the sound of a motor.

"Sure, just do it softly." I softened my voice to a whisper. "Vroom, vroom."

"Oh. How about this? *Ding, ding, ding.*"

"What's that supposed to be?"

"Firetruck," he said, pushing the red engine out of the bay doors of the fire station.

"Of course. Just do it all quietly, that's all." I left him extending the ladder of the firetruck to the split-open house, raising it to the bedroom of a tiny blue plastic boy.

It went well at first. I got right to work on the nearly finished painting on my easel, quickly moving into the rhythm and concentration of my work. Once in a while, I'd hear Timmy making hushed sounds of motors and fire sirens. *He's really being a good boy. Maybe this will work out after all.*

For me, painting takes away the world. Several hours must have passed while I tried to capture the right sheen for the hummingbird's coat. When I stepped back from the easel to look at the canvas from some distance, I felt satisfied with the morning's gift. It wasn't until I was cleaning my brush that I even remembered Timmy was in the house. Feeling a tinge of guilt for leaving him alone for so long, I laid the brush on the worktable and went downstairs to check on him.

He was still in the living room, still playing with his mini city. But the open plastic house was smudged with black soot, and I smelled something burning. Timmy was bent over the firetruck, which sat in a puddle of water. Water ran in little streams across my beautiful hardwood floors. He didn't hear me approach and jumped when I asked, "What's going on? Where'd all this water come from?"

He fell back onto his rear end, splashing into the puddle. Wet stains began creeping along the legs of his red shorts. "I was just playing."

"But what's this?" I pointed to the smoke-stained house, the plastic wrinkled in the places where the fire's heat had melted it.

"It was a fire. But don't worry. I put it out."

I stooped over and looked more closely. Inside the house, on the second floor, wedged between a plastic bed and dresser, was a votive candle with a burned-down wick.

"Did you take that candle from a drawer in the kitchen?"

He nodded.

"Where did you find matches?"

"Same place."

I snatched up the stub of a candle and a now-soggy book of matches.

"Get some paper towels and mop up this water. Hurry, before it ruins the floor."

His eyes were startled when he looked at me, as if he were surprised at the angry tone of my voice.

"Now, Timmy!"

He jumped and ran into the kitchen. I could hear him straining to reach the towels hanging over the sink, could hear paper tearing as he ripped several sheets from the roll. When he came back, he knelt on the floor and began wiping at the water, but his action just made the puddle bigger. Some of the water splashed onto my shins.

"Let me do it!" I grabbed the wad of paper towels from his hands. The morning's serenity, the joy I'd felt while painting, was gone now. "Go outside. I'll clean up this mess."

He had a hangdog look as he trudged out, letting the screen door slam after him.

On my knees, mopping water, I didn't know what to think.

Out of desperation, I called Uncle Bill's house. My cousin Chris answered the phone. She sounded weak, not like herself at all. "Things are just a mess here, Sam. I can't seem to shake this mono," she said. "Now the doctors are saying it might be something else. They're going to test me for hepatitis C."

"That's contagious, too, isn't it?"

"I guess so. I just wish they'd figure it out and make me better. I feel like shit most of the time. Mom and Dad are good about letting me stay here, but you know it's not easy living at home again. I'm used to coming and going as I want and not answering to anyone else."

Yeah, tell me about it. I hung up without asking if Uncle Bill and Aunt Millie were still thinking of taking Timmy. It was getting clearer and clearer that he might be with me for the whole summer. Just for the summer, I told myself. There was no way I was going to give up my way of life. There simply was no room in my life for a child.

Timmy came out to the kitchen wearing his red backpack and dragging his duffel bag, which was bulging with clothes. "I'm ready to go home now," he said. "I packed all my stuff, so you can take me back to my own house."

Where did he get the idea that he was going home? Didn't he understand that his father and mother weren't there? That the house was no longer his? "Timmy, you can't go home."

"How about tomorrow then?"

"No, I mean you can't go home at all. You're staying here with me for the summer."

"What about day camp? We were supposed to make a tie-dyed T-shirt and go on a field trip to the ocean."

"You might have to miss the rest of day camp. But you can sign up again next summer."

"I'm going to get bored if I don't go to camp. My dad says it's good for me to go there."

"I don't think it's going to work out this year. But let's just wait and see, okay?"

"Summer's a long time," he said, dropping the strap of his duffel bag.

And it's getting longer by the minute.

"What's going to happen after summer? What about school? I'm supposed to go into third grade. All my friends will be in third grade. Me and Darnell always get to have our desks next to each other. His last name is Watson, so we're in the same alphabet. In second grade, our desks faced each other, and when I was a little kid in first grade, our desks were side by side. Sometimes Darnell gets in trouble for talking too much. He tries to talk to me, but I don't answer because I don't want the teacher to get mad."

"Let's not worry about school," I said. "Summer just started. School's a long way off." Certainly by then, Chris would be well so that Uncle Bill and Aunt Millie could take him. Timmy wouldn't be in the same school district with his friends, but at least he'd be in Rhode Island and near what he was used to. "Take your duffel bag back to your room. The next time we go down to Clayton, we'll stop at the flea market again and pick up a dresser. Then you can put your clothes away instead of living out of a suitcase." I almost choked on that last sentence; it made his staying here seem so permanent.

Chapter 9

"If you don't have a TV, how can I plug in my PlayStation?"

"What's that?"

"It's for playing video games. Like 'Tony Hawk's Pro Skater' and 'Backyard Baseball.' I've got PlayStation 2 at home, and sometimes I take it to Grandma's."

"I don't see any need for video games or a TV or a DVD player," I said. "There's plenty to do here without artificial stimulus."

"Like what?" Timmy asked. "What am I supposed to do stuck out here in the woods all by myself?"

"Go outside and see how many birds you can spot. Maybe you'll see the deer that feeds out in the meadow. Have you ever seen a real deer before?"

He shrugged his shoulders. "My school went on a field trip to the Roger Williams Park Zoo, and I saw lots of animals."

"That's not the same as watching them in their own habitat."

"I don't care. What's the big deal, anyway? A deer's just a deer. I don't even want to see one."

I was losing patience. And thinking about the work I could be doing in the studio. I gave it one last effort. "How about building something? There's pieces of scrap wood in the woodshed, and you could build a birdhouse."

There was a glimmer of interest in his eyes. "Could I use a hammer?"

"Do you know how to use it?"

"I watched my dad. He's got a workbench in the basement, and he makes lots of stuff. He made me a toy box that looks like a racing car. He let me pound in the nails, and I even helped him paint it. We made it red with black racing stripes."

It pleased me to hear that Dan had been artistic in his own way. There was so much about my brother I didn't know. "Okay," I said. "There's a box of nails on the workbench and a hammer hanging on pegboard behind the bench. Just put it back when you're done. And don't leave any nails in the grass where I'll run over them with the riding lawnmower."

"I promise," he said as he went out the door, letting the screen slam shut.

There, that should keep him entertained for a while.

Suddenly, the door slammed again and Timmy came back in, carrying one of my hand-painted *No Hunting* signs. "What are these for? There's a whole bunch of them out there."

In all the chaos of the last few weeks, I'd nearly forgotten about the signs. I took it from him and held it up. "Can you read it?"

"No hunt-ing. No tres, tres…"

"Trespassing. That means stay away."

"Who do you want to stay away?"

"Anybody who wants to carry a gun and shoot animals." I thought of Bernice and her son-in-law and the local men who had tramped through my woods the previous fall. And, of course, I thought of Garret Belling. "I don't want people coming here who don't belong here."

"Do I belong? I'm not trespassing, am I?"

"You belong here, Timmy." I meant temporarily, but I didn't tell him that. "You're family."

"My friend has 'Big Game Hunter' for his PlayStation, and him and me shoot at deer."

"That's a game. That's different than real life." Maybe it wasn't different after all. Why plant the idea in kids' minds that it was okay to kill? A sense of relief flooded me that I didn't own a TV and Timmy couldn't play violent video games here. "I have an idea," I said. "Let's hang these up. It's a nice day for a hike through the woods." He didn't seem interested until I said, "You can carry the hammer and pound nails into trees to hold the signs."

Timmy started out as a real trouper, but soon he began to lag behind. I had to keep urging him to move on to the next spot. It took longer to post my land with him helping than it had taken when I worked alone. He wasn't used to being in the woods, and the mosquitoes and black flies bothered him, though I'd sprayed us both with repellant. I positioned a sign against a tree while Timmy stood on tiptoes and pounded nails to hold it. He liked pounding at first, but before long, the hammer seemed heavy in his hand. I usually ended up taking over for the last few nails on each sign. And he whined. "Are we almost done?" he asked at least a dozen times. We finally quit with only half my land posted.

"You never give up, do you?" Jean said when she saw the signs. I'd just gotten Timmy to bed when she stopped by on her way home from the store. She must have spotted one of the signs in her headlights as she was coming into our drive.

"Don't hassle me about this, Jean. I'm too damn tired to argue."

"Well, put it on your agenda for another day because we're sure not through discussing this." She handed me my mail she'd picked up at the post office in Clayton.

"Wait until Bernice sees those signs. And the other locals. You'll be in deep shit, Samantha."

I thought about my day with Timmy, about the gallery waiting for my work, about the nearly finished canvas standing on the easel overhead in the loft. "I already am," I said as I saw her out the door.

In addition to the latest issue of *ARTnews* and the usual assortment of junk mail, there was a letter for Timmy from my mother. He'd be happy to see it in the morning. I set it on the table, propped up against the sugar bowl so he'd spot it while he was eating breakfast. I thumbed through the rest of the mail. Some legal papers from Dan's attorney that I'd have to fill out as his representative for probate. I slipped them into a folder I kept for Dan's estate. The rest was advertising and magazines. I dropped the ads into the wastebasket and carried *ARTnews* to bed.

Once in bed, I called Kate to say good night. We had already talked by phone once that day, but it was getting so that I couldn't fall asleep without hearing her voice.

Jean was right. Bernice was really angry about the signs. When she showed up at my door, she asked, "Does this mean my son-in-law Harry and I are not allowed to come onto your land to hunt?" She always said his name that way, "my son-in-law Harry."

Timmy was within earshot, so I tried to deflect the conversation. "We'll talk about it later, Bernice," I said. "Hunting season's a long way off."

"You're right we'll talk about it. And I won't be the only one who'll want some say in the matter. Folks around here have been hunting this part of Hurricane Mountain as long as I can remember. They don't want some outsider coming in here and changing things."

"Who was that?" Timmy asked when Bernice left in a huff, walking back up the lane toward her camp.

"Just Bernice."

"Is she mad at you?"

"Look, you got a letter from Grandma." I pointed toward the sugar bowl on the table as I turned toward the cupboard to get a box of cereal.

He grabbed the envelope and tore it open, ripping off a corner of stationery in his haste. "I can read this by myself," Timmy said. "Grandma prints to make the words easier to read." He took a few bites of Raisin Bran as he was reading, but he put the spoon down as soon as he finished the letter. His bowl was still nearly full, and he hadn't touched his orange juice. "I'm not hungry," he said. "I got a tummy ache."

"Do you want to lie down a while?" I asked. "Maybe that would make the tummy ache go away."

He nodded and left in the direction of his bedroom.

I dumped his cereal out and put his glass of juice in the fridge. Then I read the letter from my mother:

Dear Timmy,

I miss you a lot, dear. Every day I think about you. Remember the time we went to the park and a chipmunk came up to the picnic

*table and ate some potato chips right out of your bag? I miss
going to the park with you. Be a good boy for Aunt Samantha.*
  Hugs and kisses,
  Grandma

Oh great, I thought. My mother was helping the situation a
lot. And then leaving it all up to me to handle. I finished a cup of
tea before going into Timmy's room. He was huddled up in a fetal
position, facing the wall. "Timmy," I said, standing over his bed,
"I think we should go to Clayton and try to find a dresser for your
room. The flea market is today, and we might find just what we're
looking for. What do you think?"

He rubbed his eyes with his fist. "Grandma didn't say anything
about me going home. I thought she was going to tell me she was
feeling better and I could go to her house now."

"I think I'll take my swimsuit when I go to Clayton in case I
decide to go to the beach. Are you coming along?"

"I guess so," Timmy mumbled as he pushed himself off the
bed.

At her cottage, Kate seemed pleased to see us, though I think
we interrupted her at work. She came to the door with a pencil
behind her ear and a sheaf of papers in her hand. She graciously
invited us in, laying her hand on my arm for a moment before
tousling Timmy's hair. After excusing herself to deposit the
article on a desk in the corner of the living room, Kate offered to
make lemonade. "Have you played Monopoly lately, Timmy?"
she asked as she filled our glasses.

"I don't think Aunt Sam likes to play games," he said, giving
me a sideways glance.

"She's probably just rusty at it." Kate handed him a ginger
snap. "She hasn't had any little boys around to play with. I'll tell
you what. Let me take you outside and show you the frog that
hangs around near the shore."

Timmy gulped his lemonade, then followed Kate out the door,
chewing his cookie. "How big is the frog?" I heard him ask her.

"About two or three inches, I'd say. You can see for
yourself."

Kate came back inside after a few minutes. "That should keep him occupied for a little while," she said, sitting beside me on the couch. Placing one hand on my thigh, she looked at me closely. "You don't seem yourself, Sam."

"How could I? Everything in my life has changed."

"I know it's a big adjustment to have the care of a child."

"Yeah, tell me about it."

"Is there anything I can do that would make you feel better? I can't change the circumstances, but I can offer you a glass of wine, a neck rub...."

I remembered the touch of her hands when she'd rubbed suntan lotion on my back that day at the beach. "A neck massage sounds good."

"Turn around then."

I shifted so that my back was to her.

"That's good," she said as she placed her hands on the nape of my neck. Her thumbs began kneading the tendons. "You're tight."

"Mmm." I shook my head from side to side, trying to loosen up. As she worked her thumbs in circles at the base of my skull, I felt the stiffness begin to ease up.

Kate's hands moved down, rubbing in long strokes across the top of my shoulders. She pressed on a spot that felt especially tight. "You're really holding tension here," she said, massaging gently.

Everything I'd held in for the last month began, at least for the moment, to melt away. Right then I knew what I wanted. Kate. I wanted her hands all over me. And her lips. I wanted her to kiss me as she had that night under the stars. I ached to be covered in her sweet breath. How I yearned to turn and face her, put my arms around her, pull us both down onto the soft couch.

The screen door slammed and Timmy came running into the cottage. "It got away," he shouted.

I was in a daze at Kate's touch. It took me a minute to realize Timmy must mean the frog.

"Oh, well," Kate said to Timmy, letting her hands drop from my shoulders. "It'll be back. That frog has been hanging around here all summer."

Timmy crawled up into a blue La-Z-Boy with a scowl on his face. "What do we do now?"

I knew what I wanted to do, but it involved just Kate and me. With a sigh, I said, "We brought our swimsuits. Is the swimming any good in front of the cottage, Kate?"

"It's perfect for kids. Nice sandy bottom. There's a few weeds, but the water stays shallow a long way out."

We changed and went outside. Kate had put on the neon pink swimsuit, and I had a hard time taking my eyes from her long lean body. At the shore, Timmy seemed timid at first, but after a little prodding, he tested the water with his toe. Soon Kate and I waded into the lake, and Timmy trailed behind us. I couldn't help but think of the last time she and I had been swimming and how romantic it had seemed.

Suddenly, Kate yelled, "Get wet!" and hit the water with the flat of her hand so that it splashed onto Timmy's belly. He didn't join in with her laughter, but he splashed her back. Before long, we were all splashing each other, chasing one another, and swimming like dolphins. To look at Timmy a half hour later, drying off with a huge beach towel, he seemed like any other kid enjoying a summer day.

After we changed back into our clothes, Kate went with us to the flea market on our search for a dresser. In addition to the usual used items on tables, crafts were displayed under tent awnings: stenciled T-shirts, tie-dyed bandannas; carved gnomes, dustpans with outdoor scenes painted on them; kitchen towels with knit tops. Kate admired some handmade jewelry, and I talked her into buying a pair of silver earrings that she seemed to particularly like. "Do something nice for yourself."

She raised an eyebrow. "You're one to give advice."

"I do feel like quite the martyr lately." I watched Timmy pawing through a crate of used toys.

"What are you going to get for yourself?"

"A book?" I suggested, pointing to the table of used paperbacks. Amid a multitude of romance and mystery, Kate discovered Carson McCuller's "Member of the Wedding." I bought that and a copy of Annie Dillard's "Pilgrim at Tinker Creek" for a grand total of seventy-five cents. Before we left, I handed over another eight dollars to a bald man who was selling furniture out of the back of his flatbed truck. Timmy wasn't impressed with the yellow dresser, but it was serviceable and cheap.

I placated him by letting him run over to Jean's store to buy a paddleball that he'd spotted when we were there. I didn't go in with him because I didn't want to listen to Jean harping at me about the signs. Timmy came back out the door bouncing the paddleball, and he was still bouncing it when I dropped him and Kate off at the Clayton Inn. She was going to treat him to an ice cream cone on the porch of the inn, then they'd walk to her cottage for another swim. I'd complained to Kate about how frustrated I was with trying to get my painting project done, and she'd offered to keep Timmy for the rest of the day. I waved to them as I drove off with the yellow dresser sticking out of the Jeep's backseat.

Bless you, Kate. I drove up the mountain, the top down, the wind blowing my hair. Oh, these moments of quiet—I'd never realized how precious they were.

When I reached my cabin, it didn't take long for me to climb the stairs to my studio and sink into my own glorious world. It was just the time I needed to finish the hummingbird painting. Satisfied, I wrote *Samantha Warren* in the lower corner. Hours had passed while I worked, and I had to admit in all that time, I didn't give one thought to Timmy.

Chapter 10

"You've got to take me home." Timmy stood outside the fence that enclosed the garden patch and protected it from deer. His fingers clung onto the wire mesh.

I was inside the fence, kneeling and weeding the peas and bush beans. We'd been over this before, so I ignored him. Sticking the trowel into the dirt, I pried up another weed.

He insisted, "Grandma misses me."

I sat back on my heels. "I know Grandma misses you. We'll go to visit her sometime, but not now."

"I don't want to visit her, I want to stay there. I need to go back to Providence."

"That's not possible," I said as I returned to weeding. *If he only knew that I want that as much as he does.*

He kicked at the fence with his sneaker, then turned and stormed back into the cabin. Later, I found that he had become mute. He'd decided not to talk; his lips were sealed. I discovered this when I asked him what he wanted for lunch. He answered me only with body signals or a movement of his head. No, he didn't want tuna fish—a shake of the head. Yes, he wanted peanut butter and jelly—a nod.

I cut the sandwich in two and placed it on a plate in front of him. He nibbled at one half, holding it with both hands, a gob of grape jelly sticking to the side of his mouth. When there was just crust left, uneven as if it had been cut with pinking shears, he put it on his plate. Then he followed the same ritual with the second half, and when there was only crust left, stained purple with jelly and greasy with peanut butter, he set it down and pushed his plate away.

85

"Do you want a glass of milk?" I asked.

He nodded, so I poured a tumbler of cold milk and handed it to him. He shook his head and tapped the edge of the glass with his finger. Then he made a movement as if he were pouring something into the glass.

"I don't get it," I said, and I could hear exasperation in my voice. "You have to tell me."

Timmy rose from the table and got a small can of Hershey's syrup from the shelf on the refrigerator door. He dumped a thick stream of the dark chocolate into his glass, then he looked up at me and made a stirring motion over the glass with his index finger.

"A spoon?"

He nodded, and I handed him a teaspoon from the silverware drawer. As Timmy stirred, he watched the dark liquid swirl into the white milk. When he finished drinking, downing the whole glass in huge gulps, there was a brown mustache over his lip.

I made a motion of moving my finger over my own lip to let him know he should wipe it off. *Cut it out, Sam,* I scolded myself, *you're just playing into his game.*

Even the swing that I hung on the tall oak behind the cabin didn't induce Timmy to speak. "Hop on and I'll push you." I held a thick strand of rope in each hand. He backed onto the wide board that I'd notched and positioned between the ropes. "Does that feel comfortable?"

He nodded.

"Here we go." I felt the unforgiving hardness of his back as I placed my hands between his shoulder blades. At first Timmy seemed timid, allowing only a few gentle shoves. But as he grew in confidence, I pushed harder.

The ropes squeaked on the limb of the oak tree. I stepped out of the way to watch him moving back and forth, his feet pumping. I thought he was enjoying it, but when I caught a glance of his face, I saw that he was scowling and his lips were set in a hard and determined line.

After a day of awkward signs with his hands and movements

of the head in place of language, I grew frustrated with Timmy's antics. I thought back over the time that Timmy had been with me and tried to remember what, if anything, had gotten a positive response from him. Badger. He'd responded to Jean's dog.

I called the store to talk to Jean, but Robby answered. He said she'd left early and that he and Julie, another of the summer help, were going to close for her.

"Do you know where she was going?" I asked. "Was she coming home?"

"I didn't ask her. She just said for us to close up at 9:00."

Glancing at the clock next to the refrigerator, I saw that it was only 7:10 pm. Jean had covered the busy late afternoon and supper crowd. I knew that sometimes if the evening seemed slow, she left early. But I didn't know if she'd be coming home. I'd have to wing it on my own with Timmy.

He was busy with his Matchbox cars and buildings. As I passed him in the living room, I cringed at the black smudges and wilted plastic on the toy house, reminders of the fire Timmy had set. I made myself comfortable on the futon couch. "Pilgrim at Tinker Creek" was lying on the coffee table that Jean had made from a slab of pine tree. I picked up the book from the glossy, varnished surface and found the dog-eared page where I'd left off.

I was reading when Timmy poked my arm. I didn't pay much attention. I was tired of trying to coax him to talk. "Go back to playing with your cars," I said. "I want to read now."

I'd just turned the page when I felt a tugging at the hem of my shorts. I glanced up to see Timmy patting his belly.

"If you're hungry," I said, "go get some graham crackers from the cupboard." I returned to reading.

When he jabbed my thigh, I didn't bother to look up. "You can have a small glass of milk with it," I said, assuming that was what he wanted.

When he kicked my shin with his sneaker, I dropped the book onto my lap. What?" I said with annoyance.

Timmy was bent forward slightly, rubbing his belly in fast circles.

"If you won't talk to me, I don't know what you want."

He poked at his belly.

"Does it hurt?"

He nodded.

"When did it start hurting?"

He shrugged his shoulders.

I set the book on the coffee table and fetched a bottle of Pepto-Bismol from the medicine cabinet. "Take some of this. It'll make your tummy feel better."

He leaned forward and wrapped his mouth around the spoonful of pink liquid that I held out to him.

"Now lie down for a while on the couch and see if that helps."

Wordlessly, he climbed up onto the futon.

I'd lost my interest in reading. Instead, I went into the kitchen and was making a cup of tea for myself when Jean's truck passed on the way to her cabin. I waited until she was home and called her. When I explained over the phone that Timmy might perk up if he saw Badger, she said, "Bring him over. Badger needs some exercise."

Timmy seemed to forget about his tummy ache when he saw the dog. And Badger seemed just as happy to have a boy to play with. Jean handed Timmy an old tennis ball. "This is Badger's favorite toy," she said. "Throw it, and he'll go fetch it. Want me to show you how?"

Timmy shook his head and reached for the ball. We watched him lob it through the air. Sure enough, Badger went bounding after it and carried it in his mouth back to Timmy. Timmy patted the dog's head, took the drool-wet ball from his mouth, and tossed it again.

Jean and I left them to their game of toss-and-fetch and went inside. Her cabin was much larger and more spacious than mine. She got herself a cold Miller Lite and a Pepsi for me. We carried them out to the back deck, which had an amazing view of the mountains. Jean plopped into a canvas chair and propped her feet onto the deck railing. "What's wrong with the boy? He seems okay to me."

"He refuses to talk." I told her how Timmy had been mum all day.

"Kid stuff." She gulped her beer. "He'll get over it. How are you doing?"

"I'm exhausted. I'm just not used to having a kid around. And I miss being able to do my own work whenever I want. I'm getting way behind in my painting."

"Yeah. When winter comes, I can get back to my woodcarving. It's pretty much on hold during tourist season."

Woodcarving was too simple a way to put what Jean created. Her pieces were exquisite: she began with a tree root or a piece of driftwood and worked with its natural form, carving until it was transformed into a child floating in a mother's womb or two female lovers wrapped in an embrace or a voluptuous woman stretching her arms to the sky. Another kind of carving she did began with a tree burl. She hollowed the burl into a bowl or cup or vase, following its natural rounded shape and polishing the wood to a gleam.

"Store's busy, huh?"

"Crazy. But that's what brings in the bucks. And talking about bucks, the four-legged kind…"

"Let's not get into that tonight."

"Okay, not tonight. Just so you know I'm still pissed about those damn signs."

"Yeah, yeah, yeah. You and half of Maine, I guess."

"That shouldn't surprise you." Jean took another swig of beer and crossed her ankles on the railing. "Did someone else complain? Did Bernice get after you about posting your land?"

"She made it clear that she doesn't like it. And either she or someone else is trying to get me to back down."

"What do you mean?"

I explained about the incidents: finding the torn signs and coming upon the skinned raccoon.

"I told you posting the land would bring trouble. Like you said, it sounds like someone's trying to scare you so you'll change your mind. It's just bullying tactics. Tell you the truth, though, I wouldn't mind if it worked so that you'd give up that idiotic idea of yours."

I had to ask. "You didn't have a hand in it, did you?"

Her feet dropped from the railing and she sat upright in the lawn chair, her eyes blazing. "Sam, how can you even think that? You know damn well if I've got a problem with something you do, I'm going to talk to you about it face to face, none of this behind-the-back shit."

"That's what I figured."

"I don't like what you're doing and I'll do everything I can to get you to change your mind, but I'll do it upfront. After all these years of being friends, you think I'd do something to hurt you?"

The sounds of Badger barking and Timmy laughing floated to us from the front yard. I thought back on the years Jean and I had spent as friends in college and her offer to sell me the cabin and land at such a good price. "Jean," I said, rubbing her back, "forget I even said that, okay?"

She looked into my eyes for a minute, then she grinned. "Forget what?" And I knew it would never be mentioned again.

We watched an incredible sunset over the mountains before moving inside to play cribbage. Timmy sat at the table with us, Badger asleep under the table with his paws resting on his feet. Timmy still wasn't speaking, but he seemed lighter in mood and smiled whenever he reached down to scratch Badger's neck. We began to teach him how to count the cards and peg the holes, and he found that he had to talk if he wanted to play. Soon he was adding up his cards and calling out his hand. "Fifteen two, fifteen four, and a pair makes ..." He paused to calculate in his head. "Six?"

That's right," Jean said. "Peg six holes."

I didn't comment on his talking, but I let Jean know I was relieved by making eye contact with her over the table.

Jean set out a bowl of potato chips, which we all dug into. She had another beer, while Timmy and I drank Pepsi. I'd nearly forgotten how much I enjoyed Jean's company when we avoided the issue that divided us. After she won two hands and skunked us on the third, I said to Timmy, "Don't worry. She always wins."

Jean scooped up the cards, wrapping a rubber band around

them. She slipped the pegs into a compartment on the back of the cribbage board, then set the board and the deck of cards on a shelf over the table. "That's why Sam keeps playing against me," she said to Timmy. "She thinks one of these times she's going to win."

By the time we got ready to leave, it was dark outside. When we stepped out the door, Timmy held back. "Come on," I prodded. "We need to get home—it's past your bedtime."

He looked out at the vast blackness, broken only by the outside lamp over Jean's door, the light over my door in the distance, and stars punctuating the sky. "I'm afraid," he said in a small voice.

"Afraid of what?" I asked.

He stood on the threshold. "It's so dark out there."

I tried to see it through his eyes: no streetlights illuminating the way, no lamps glowing from neighbors' windows, no headlights beaming from cars on the street.

"Would you like Badger to walk you home?" Jean asked him. "That dog's real brave. The dark doesn't bother him at all."

"Okay," Timmy said.

"Call him then."

"Come here, boy," Timmy crooned, patting his knees, and Badger leapt out from under the table.

I let Timmy hold the flashlight, and he held onto the dog's collar as we walked. When we reached my cabin, I blinked my outside light so Jean would know we'd made it. We heard her whistle, and Badger bounded on home.

Timmy went willingly to bed. I sat on the futon to read, then checked on him a half hour later. He was out to the world, hugging the long-neglected toy dog that looked like Badger.

Watching him sleep, his face buried in the pillow, his blond hair mussed up, I realized how innocent and vulnerable Timmy was. After all, he was just a little boy, and he'd lost everything he knew and loved. He didn't have his father and mother anymore. I wondered what it must feel like to be so young and so alone in the world. Then I had a terrifying thought: what if he had been with his parents in the car when it crashed? I sat down on his bed and placed my hand on his back, feeling the rhythm of his breathing.

Right then, I made a vow to myself. I would try harder.

I left his door open a crack and collapsed on the futon, too tired to lift my book from the coffee table and pick up where I'd left off reading. In a state of fatigue, my resolve began to weaken. I wondered: *Is this what it's going to be like with Timmy here? Trials and tribulations to get through every day?*

Chapter 11

The faces came to me in a dream. I'd been thinking of making a series of paintings on the theme of secrets women find necessary to keep to themselves. I'd been struggling with how to go about it, and there it was all laid out for me while I slept. In the dream, I saw that each painting would be the portrait of a different woman, and her eyes would suggest some mystery that would never be fully revealed, no matter how long and hard the viewer looked at the painting.

Coming awake with excitement burning in my belly, I sat up in bed, turned on the light, and reached for the small sketchpad and pencil I kept on the bedside table. With the pad propped against my raised knees, I made quick sketches and notes.

In my mind, I saw the women I wanted to paint, each in a different posture and setting. The one thing they would have in common would be mysterious eyes. After sketching for several hours, I set the pad and pencil down and drifted back to sleep with the images of women cramming my mind.

A few hours later, I woke to a day swathed in light. Timmy was in the kitchen fixing his breakfast, but I was hungry in a different way. I dressed quickly in a loose-woven shirt and khaki shorts, slipped my feet into sandals, and ducked my head into the kitchen to check on Timmy. "Did you remember that Jean's taking you down to the store with her today?"

He looked up at me, his face beaming. "Yep. I have to look after Badger. He gets lonely while Jean's working. That's what she told me."

Just then, there was the beep of a horn and the quick bark of a dog. "Sounds like they're here," I said. "You all set to go?"

He dropped his spoon into his cereal bowl and wiped milk from his mouth. "Yep." He sprinted toward the door.

"Just a minute." I grabbed his shirt as he went by.

"What?" he asked, impatience in his voice.

"You do whatever Jean tells you." With my thumb, I wiped a drop of milk from his chin. "And be a good boy for her."

"I will." He dashed out the door, and I soon heard the truck door slam shut and Jean backing out of the driveway.

The whole morning stretched out in front of me, and I felt almost giddy with the luxury of solitude. Grabbing a bottle of water and a bagel from the fridge, I started up the stairs to the loft. After a few steps, I turned back and went into the kitchen to set the timer on the stove. I didn't trust myself to remember to pick Timmy up at noon otherwise.

I looked around my studio and began to doubt myself. What was I thinking? With Timmy here for the summer, how could I even think about starting a series of paintings? Yet, here it was, burning in my mind—these portraits of women whose eyes stared out at the world, eyes hinting at some trouble lurking just below the surface.

There would be tension in the paintings; I'd have to figure out how to express that. It might work best to use a conventional color palette. The body of each individual woman would be stiff, her head sitting rigidly on her neck. The shoulders would be square and broad so that, along with the head and torso, the body suggested a cross. Swirling under the self-confident stance, however, would be a confusion of emotions barely held in. The secret each woman kept to herself would have to be conveyed through the eyes. At first viewing, the eyes would seem transparent to the viewer so that he would feel he could see right through to her soul. But as he gazed longer at her, he'd see that they were opaque. Painting the eyes would be my greatest challenge.

How many women did I want in the series? Six seemed like the right number. One painting could be of a woman sitting in a chair, maybe a wicker chair, something that didn't appear quite substantial enough to hold her. There'd be an opened book on the floor at her feet. She might have her knees drawn up and be clutching her ankles. One of the paintings would be of a woman smoking. She'd hold the cigarette between two fingers, and they would indicate a tinge of nicotine stain. She'd be wearing a sweater with a high neck, the knitted fabric in folds around her face. The cuffs of the sleeves would reach her knuckles, so that just the fingers holding the cigarette would be exposed. Would she have a hat on her head? Yes, a beret. Black? No. Red. Everything else in the painting would be black—her hair, her brooding eyes, her clothing. But there'd be those two points of red: the tip of the cigarette and the beret.

Excited, the ideas bursting from my mind, I taped large pieces of paper to a blank canvas on the easel and blocked out these tentative portraits. Another woman came to me. This one would be sitting on a boulder with the branch of a white pine casting a shadow on her face. Her bare toes would be poised in green tufts of grass that grew up around the gray boulder. She'd be leaning forward slightly, chin resting on her folded hands, elbows on her knees. The eyes would be pensive.

Suddenly, I had an idea for another painting. This one would be of a woman wearing a white shawl. The shawl covers her head and drapes down over her shoulder; one hand clutches the edge of the shawl near her breast. Maybe the other hand is near her waist. And there's something different about this painting in the series— we don't see her eyes at all. Her whole face is hidden in the dark cave of the shawl, and the viewer has no chance of learning her secret. The only hint is the hand resting on the slightly swollen belly.

The timer going off downstairs made me jump. Could it already be time to pick up Timmy at Jean's store? It seemed like I'd just started to work. Feeling resentful for being interrupted, I stepped back and looked at the rough drawings I'd made. The work was going so well. If only I had time to keep at it.

When I stopped for Timmy at The Village Store, he gave Badger such a passionate goodbye hug that it seemed impossible to tear him away from the dog's neck. "It's too bad you don't want to come with me," I said. "I'm driving to Fredericksville for the afternoon. I think I remember seeing a McDonald's there." That was the secret word to release his grasp on the dog. He didn't know my real reason for going to Fredericksville was to buy painting supplies.

First, we crossed the street to pick up the mail. Miss Helen was delighted to see that I had someone with me. "And who's this little fella?" she asked as she handed me a few letters. I explained that he was my nephew from Rhode Island.

"Come to Clayton for a visit?" Miss Helen asked Timmy, but he hung close behind me and didn't answer. She turned to me again. "Is he staying with you for the whole summer?"

"We don't know yet how long Timmy will be here," I said quickly. I could see that Miss Helen wanted more of the story, but I cut her off by saying we were on our way to Fredericksville and turned to leave.

"Wait, Samantha. There's a package that came in care of you." She smiled at Timmy and said, "It's addressed to *Master Timothy Warren*. I wondered who that was, and now I know." She reached under the counter and brought out a small box, wrapped in brown paper from a grocery bag and sealed with masking tape. I knew immediately that it was from my mother without even looking at the return address.

Miss Helen handed it over the counter to Timmy, and he had to reach on his tiptoes to take it. "What is it?" he asked me, holding the box to his ear and shaking it.

"Something from Grandma, I think."

"Can I open it?"

"When we get in the Jeep and on our way. Say goodbye to Miss Helen." He tossed a glance in her direction but didn't say anything.

"I hope you come by again, young man. But I can't promise to have a package for you every time." Miss Helen chuckled.

Timmy sat in the front seat, patiently holding the box in his lap as we drove out of Clayton in the opposite direction of Hurricane Mountain. Once we were on the road to Fredericksville, he asked, "I want to open it now, Aunt Sam. You said."

I nodded, and he tore into the package, ripping off the brown paper and letting it fall to the floor of the Jeep. Glancing over, I could see that it was a Whitman's sampler chocolate box. I waited for a squeal of appreciation when he opened the box, but he silently put the lid back in place.

"Did Grandma send you some candy?"

"Nope."

"Something else in the box?"

He stared down at the lid and spoke in flat monosyllables. "Yep."

"Well, what is it?"

"Nothing."

"There's got to be something in it." I hung onto the wheel as the road made a sharp curve. "What is it?"

"I'll show you later." He looked out the side window as we passed Hills Pond; a man about his father's age was fishing alone in a rowboat.

We drove the rest of the way to Fredericksville, where I treated Timmy to a Happy Meal at McDonald's. He left the Whitman's box on the seat of the Jeep, but I'd grabbed it and stuck it in my pocket before we went inside the fast-food restaurant. I'd never seen a kid enjoy a meal as much as he did this one. He dipped his fries one by one into a small paper cup of ketchup, and you would have thought he was dipping a cracker into caviar. He sipped at his Sprite as if it were fine wine. After he devoured his cheeseburger, savoring every bite, he unwrapped the toy that came with the meal. He twirled the blades of the small plastic helicopter with his finger. "Neat," he said, lifting the helicopter over his head, then landing it on the table.

He played with it while I finished my salad and coffee, then I said, "I bet the present Grandma sent is neat, too."

He shrugged his shoulders and lifted the helicopter into the air again.

I pulled the box out of my pocket and set it on the table between us. "Why don't you show me what's in here?"

Timmy stood up on his bench and swooped the helicopter in circles.

"Sit down, Timmy, before you fall."

He plunked into his seat. "What?"

"Show me what's in the box that Grandma mailed you."

"You can open it." He went back to playing with his toy. I lifted the lid and gasped when I saw my brother's silver watch lying in a bed of facial tissues. It had been a gift to Dan from my mother at his graduation from Brown, and even though Dan had bought himself better watches over the years, he'd still worn this one often. What had my mother been thinking to send it to Timmy now? Maybe when he was older, he'd appreciate it. But surely now it would just bring back painful memories. "Your daddy's watch," I said. I took the silver band out of the box and checked the face for the time: it was correct at 1:33.

"Grandma must've sent the wrong box. Why would I want that old thing?"

I finished my coffee and set it on the tray with the dirty napkins and ketchup-smeared cheeseburger wrapper. "Maybe she thought you'd like to have something of your dad's."

Timmy scooted out from the table. "Can we go now?"

"Empty this into the trash," I said, pushing the tray toward him.

As he carried our litter over to the trash bin, I picked up the watch, leaving the empty box on the table.

Chapter 12

A few days later, the weather was so pleasant that I convinced Timmy to go for a walk. At the spring, I showed him how to cup water and sip it from his hands. Along the trail, we found puffballs on the ground, and I demonstrated how to stomp on them so that dust flew up. Then we hiked to the Bailey field where he got a big kick out of climbing in and out of the cellar hole. He was amazed that a house used to stand there. As we continued walking down the mountain, I heard a loud drumming sound and pointed out a pileated woodpecker boring holes in an old birch tree.

"It looks like Woody Woodpecker," Timmy said.

"That's because it has a red crest on its head." We watched the large bird working like a jackhammer, drilling a sizeable hole into the decayed tree.

"What's it doing?"

"Looking for insects to eat. Oh, look here." I pointed out claw marks in the bark of a beech tree. "A bear did that."

"You got bears here?"

"Sure. But they're black bears, not grizzlies. They usually won't hurt a human."

"I don't want to see any bears."

Farther down the mountain, we reached the back line of my property. Something blue caught my eye through the trees. I hurried on to examine it and discovered a small tent: one of those light, nylon tents that set up so easily and have room for four people at the most.

"Wow, what's that?" Timmy asked. "It looks like a little house. It's somebody's tent, isn't it?"

I was furious at this discovery. Who would have the audacity to

99

set up a tent on private property? "It's a tent all right," I barked.

"Are you mad, Aunt Sam? You sound mad."

"You bet! I'm spitting mad that someone put up a tent on my property."

We moved closer to investigate. A small, shallow fire pit had been dug about ten feet in front of the tent, and there were ashes in it. I reached my hand into the pit and let some of the ashes sift through my fingers—they were cold, so there had not been a fire here recently. A log lying on its side served as a seat near the fire pit. Drag marks in the earth indicated that someone had moved the log there intentionally.

Hanging on a nail in a pine tree was a long ladle for dipping water. A cast iron skillet hung from another nail, and a pot for boiling water was turned upside down on the ground. Huddled next to the tent was an army green metal trunk with a padlock on its latch. I jiggled the lock, trying to open the trunk, but it was secured fast.

Unzipping the flap of the tent, I stuck my head inside. Timmy crawled between my legs and stuck his head into the tent. It smelled musty as if it hadn't been used for a couple of days, but there was plenty of evidence to indicate that someone had been living here in the not too distant past. A down sleeping bag lay along one side of the tent, an army blanket wadded up at one end for a pillow. Two flashlights were next to the sleeping bag—one was a red lantern type with a square body and the other was a cylindrical army green one that took D batteries.

"Look at all this stuff. Is someone living here?" Timmy asked.

"Somebody's been spending some time here, that's for sure." I stepped around Timmy into the tent. The dome ceiling was low, and I had to stoop. I saw a clear plastic box that held wax candles and matches, then I turned over a coffee can and found a roll of toilet tissue.

"Geez," Timmy said as he scooted into the tent, "even got toilet paper."

He helped me with my snooping, and we found cans of soup stacked in a small pyramid. Lying next to the soup were a can opener, a plastic dish, and a steel utensil that looked like a fork, spoon, and knife all in one. A propane stove was folded up with the lid pulled securely down and latched. There was no sign of fresh food left out to attract animals. Whoever had been staying here was no novice to living in the woods.

I didn't think I'd ever find myself knocking on the door at Bernice Slade's cabin. But here I was with Timmy in tow on her front stoop. When she opened the door, she seemed surprised to see me. She leaned against the doorframe, her arms folded, her painted nails tapping her forearms, which were densely freckled after many years in the sun. I tried to keep my eyes from the vee neckline of her top, which revealed twin bulges of freckled breasts.

"Samantha Warren. You've been on the mountain for well over a year, and you finally drop in for a neighborly call," she said.

"Bernice, I wanted to ask you something."

"Good afternoon to you, too."

My first impulse was to retort with a snide remark, but she was right to call me on my lack of manners. I made myself slow down to allow for chit-chat. "Seems especially hot this summer, don't you think?"

Her eyes creased as a smile flickered across her face. "Humid too," she said. I could smell beer on her breath. The way she smiled, her red lipstick etching the fine wrinkles around her lips, made it obvious that she was enjoying my discomfit. "You're probably used to air conditioning where you come from."

"Well, we really need it in the city."

"This is a long way from the city. Folks make do around here." She seemed to like to take every chance she could to remind me that I was an outsider on Hurricane Mountain.

My attempt at small talk was not accomplishing what I'd set out to do, which was to appear friendly so I could gather information about the camper in my woods. I switched tactics. "Bernice, I want you to meet my nephew, Timmy. He's visiting me for a while."

101

Her eyes moved to Timmy, who was doing his best to hide behind me. Immediately, her eyes softened. "Visiting from where?" she asked Timmy in a gentler voice, craning her neck to see him.

Timmy remained silent behind me. "Providence, Rhode Island," I answered for him.

Just then, two boys came racing out from around the side of the cabin, whooping at each other.

"Hey, slow down there," Bernice called to them. "Can't you see we've got company?"

The boys came to a screeching halt, the taller one nearly colliding with the shorter one. During the time I'd been Bernice's neighbor, I'd seen these boys quite often, but only at a distance. From what Jean had told me, I knew their parents were Bernice's daughter and son-in-law, and they lived down the mountain in the village of Clayton. They were good-looking kids with freckled faces, but they both needed haircuts. They were wearing cut-off jeans and T-shirts that looked to be in need of laundry soap. "Who's that, Grandma?" the taller one asked.

Bernice looked down at Timmy, still lagging behind me. There was a hint of tenderness to her voice, which I had not anticipated, as she asked him, "What did you say your name was? Jimmy?"

I knew Timmy would be too shy to say, so I jumped in for him. "It's Timmy. With a *T*."

"Well, Timmy with a T, meet Jason," she pointed to the red-haired, taller boy. "He's ten."

"I'm going to be eleven next month, Grandma."

"Okay, Jason's almost eleven. And this is Cody. How old are you, Cody?" she teased.

"You know. Nine. Remember, my dad and mom gave me a BB gun for my birthday?"

Nine, I thought, *a year older than Timmy and he has a BB gun.*

Jason tossed in, "I think they're getting me a twenty-two on my next birthday."

"Not until you're twelve, Jason. That's what your mom and dad told me. Next summer's soon enough. You can target practice with your BB gun for now."

I hated the talk of guns. I couldn't imagine kids being allowed to have guns of any type. I wouldn't even buy Timmy the plastic squirt gun he'd spotted at the flea market in Clayton. I watched the boys as they eyed Timmy warily. These were not playmates I would choose for Timmy, but they were that scarce commodity around here: kids. "Timmy's visiting me from out of state," I said. "He's been lonely for someone to play with."

"He can come with us," Jason said. "We're just playing army. What do you want to be," he asked Timmy, "an army guy or a terrorist?" When Timmy just shrugged his shoulders, Jason said, "Okay you're an army guy with me. Cody's the terrorist. We've got to get him." When Cody heard that, he sprinted off toward the back of the cabin.

Jason was ready to take off, too. "You coming?" he called to Timmy over his shoulder.

I nudged Timmy with my hand. "You've been wanting to play," I said. "Now's your chance. Go catch up with them." There was a furrow of anxiety on his forehead as he built up his courage. Then he broke into a run, chasing after the other boys.

With the boys gone, I took the opportunity to approach Bernice with what I'd really come for. "There's been someone camping in my woods. Do you have any idea who it might be?"

"Oh, so that's why you're so friendly today. I should have guessed there were ulterior motives." Bernice disappeared inside the cabin. She came back with two glasses of iced tea. She handed me one, then sat down on the bench of the picnic table.

I watched her take a swig, almost smacking her lips, and I wondered if hers was laced with something stronger. "I thought you might have heard about someone hanging around up here."

"No." She shook the ice cubes in her glass and took another drink. "I can't say that I have." It was obvious that she wasn't going to tell me if she did know. This was the old Bernice, the neighbor who could be incredibly obstinate.

"Somebody's trespassing," I said, setting my full glass on the picnic table.

"Oh, I forgot. Your land's posted. Private."

"That's right. And I'm going to find out who's on it and boot him out of there."

"Sure you are. Keep everyone off your land, city girl." Bernice finished off her tea, dumped mine onto the ground, and carried the empty glasses back into the cabin, letting the door fall closed behind her.

When the boys came careening around the cabin chasing one another, I pulled Timmy away from Jason and Cody. "We're going home."

"But why, Aunt Sam? I'm having fun."

"We're leaving, and that's all there is to it."

Timmy wouldn't forgive me for tearing him away from his new friends. He sat on the swing I'd built for him and pumped his legs as hard as he could. Up he went and down and up and down. I was afraid he'd fall off the way he was soaring so far above the ground. Watching from the upstairs windows, I almost called down to him to be more careful. But then I realized he was probably trying to force the anger out of his system—anger at me for bringing him here to this mountain, anger at his parents for dying, anger at not being allowed to play with his new friends. Of course, the boys had wanted him to stay, but I certainly wasn't going to leave him with Bernice. And I didn't want a parcel of kids in my yard—I needed to try to get some work done in my studio, and for that, I needed quiet.

I checked on Timmy every once in a while from the loft window. He'd swing forward, head back, blond hair flying, feet pointed to the sky, his body suspended in a great arc of air. Then he'd kick his legs and swing back so high I was afraid he'd loop over the tree branch.

I moved back to my easel and tried to concentrate on the figure I was plotting out. I had blocked in the wicker chair she'd sit in, the space her body would take up, the angles I envisioned her sitting at. Now I needed a model, and, of course, the first person who came to mind was Kate. It would take some nerve to ask her because she had a deadline for her own project. Yet I couldn't go on without someone posing in that chair. And what a wonderful excuse to see Kate every day.

Timmy was still mad at me the next day, but he grudgingly helped me stack wood. We'd been working for a while when Bernice drove into my yard on a lime green four-wheeler. A flag with butterflies and flowers on it fluttered from the front fender. She stopped next to me and surprised me when she said, "I'm sorry about your brother and his wife. That must be hard for the little boy."

At that moment, Timmy came around the cabin, struggling with three chunks of wood in his arms. He dropped them near the neat pile I'd made and they clattered to the ground.

"Timmy," I said, still feeling off-balance by Bernice's unexpected kind remarks, "pile those logs neatly onto the stack." Timmy picked up one log and tried placing it on the pile, but he couldn't reach the top tier.

Stepping off the four-wheeler, Bernice said, "I'll give you a hand." She picked up the log that had rolled off and placed it on top. "Now you pass me those other two sticks." Timmy handed them to her one by one, and Bernice set them onto the woodpile, then lightly wiped her hands on her lavender knit pants. "There, that looks better, doesn't it?"

Timmy nodded.

"My grandsons were wondering if you wanted to go fishing with us."

I jumped in. "Maybe sometime," I said, trying to skirt the issue.

"Why not now?" Bernice asked. "The boys are itching to get down to the brook and catch some trout." She turned her attention to Timmy again. "Have you ever been fishing?"

"My daddy said he'd take me. He said he'd get me my own pole and put the worm on the hook for me. But I'm not afraid of worms."

"Well, then, you can help Jason and Cody dig for night crawlers. I'll show you how to use a pitchfork to turn up the dirt."

I pictured the tine of a pitchfork going through Timmy's

sneaker. "He should probably stay here where I can watch out for him."

"Do you think I can't watch out for him? I've been a mother and a grandmother for some time now. I've had plenty of practice at this." She turned to Timmy. "I'm sure I can find a fishing pole you can use. We'll take a walk down to the brook and see if there are any trout biting."

"You said Jason and Cody are going?" Timmy asked her.

"Of course. You think they'd let me leave them behind if there's fish to be caught?" She patted the backseat of the four-wheeler, which was upholstered with sheep's wool. "Hop on and I'll give you a ride across to my place. You can help the boys dig some crawlers, then we'll hike down to the brook. You'll be back in time for supper."

Timmy threw me a longing glance. "Please, Aunt Sam."

I felt caught in a quandary. Should I let him go? Could I trust Bernice to watch out for him? She didn't show any sign of having been drinking; her eyes were clear, and there wasn't any hint of alcohol on her breath. Also, Bernice seemed genuinely fond of her grandsons, and she seemed to have a comfortable way with kids. "Well, you've got to spray mosquito repellant on first. And you have to hold on tightly to Bernice on the four-wheeler. And wear a helmet."

"I've got one right here," Bernice said, and she produced a kid's orange bike helmet from a lattice box on the fender.

After Timmy rode off on the four-wheeler, I had three choices: sit and fret about whether he would be safe with Bernice, steal the few hours to work on my painting, or check out the anonymous camper in my woods. Worrying about Timmy would do nothing but waste time. What I wanted was to escape into my loft and pick up a paintbrush. But I was uneasy—and angry—about the tent in my back acres. I put on some sturdy hiking shoes, grabbed a pair of binoculars, and set off to investigate.

As I walked through the woods to the perimeter of my property, I tried to imagine who could have set up the tent. It wasn't teenagers, that was for sure. The evidence pointed to an experienced camper. Someone from the lumber company that owned the nearby land? No. They would know clearly the boundaries for my property line and would have approached me for permission first. Surely, it was someone who was brash enough to ignore the *No Trespassing* signs. But what was the motive? Why pitch a tent on my property when there was so much camping space available in the state park? What was the intruder looking for?

When I neared the clearing in the woods, I walked more quietly, trying not to step on any twigs that might snap and give me away. I followed along the edge of the tree line until I could see the dome shape of the blue tent. There was a figure squatting near the cold fire pit. He wore a black sweatshirt with the hood pulled over his head, so I couldn't see his features. I wasn't even sure it was a "he," but the body movements made me think it was a male.

The stranger had something in his hands, but I wasn't close enough to make it out. I lifted my binoculars and sighted in on him. I was trying to make out if it was Garret Belling, but just as I got him in my sights, he shifted so that his back was to me, concealing whatever was in his hands. He moved over to the army green metal trunk that sat beside the tent. Carefully, he laid the object inside, then he lowered the lid and snapped the padlock shut. Through the binoculars, I saw him double check that the padlock caught and was locked. He pocketed what I figured must have been a key.

I waited for him to turn around so I could get a better description. But instead he stood and walked behind the tent. Now he was completely obliterated from my sight. I expected him to return to the trunk, the fire pit, or the front of the tent—somewhere within my view. I trained the binoculars on the area where he had disappeared. Nearly twenty minutes passed before I realized he wasn't coming back. He must have gone into the woods behind the tent and vanished in the thicket.

I sat a while longer on a lichen-covered boulder while I pondered my next move. I reprimanded myself for not going up to him and demanding that he explain what he was doing on my land. But there was no telling what I might be dealing with. I wasn't about to follow him into the woods—though they were my woods! And I didn't dare venture over to the tent in case he was still around somewhere. I'd have to come back some other time to continue my investigation.

I headed back toward my cabin, walking along the old logging road. I had just entered a wooded area when I thought I heard something behind me: a rustling of leaves, snap of a twig. I stopped to listen more carefully, but the sounds stopped, too. When I took some more steps, I heard it again: that movement somewhere behind me. Was the intruder following me?

Then I heard the click of a bullet sliding into a chamber. After that, all I heard was the heavy beating of my own heart, fluttering like a wild partridge, ready to leap out of my chest. I dropped to the ground. On my hands and knees, I scurried into the brush and crouched behind a fallen spruce tree. Through the green branches, I watched closely in the direction I'd come from. Nearby a cardinal whistled, deerflies buzzed close to my head, but I didn't dare swat them. I kept as still as I could and waited.

There was a loud crack and a bullet whizzed by about ten feet over my head to the left of me. Falling to the ground, I crawled on my stomach to a large boulder and hid behind it.

My heart raced and my hands shook as I hugged the ground. I decided to stay put and prayed that whoever had fired the gun would leave soon.

The sound of footsteps seemed to come nearer, boots making a crunching noise in old leaves. I clasped my hands tightly to keep them from trembling and held my breath. The person seemed to be walking nearby, though I couldn't see him from behind the boulder. After what seemed like a long time, I heard the footsteps moving away. I waited until I couldn't hear anything anymore, then I waited ten or fifteen minutes longer. When I stood up, no one was in sight.

"Maybe you just imagined it," Jean said. I'd called her at work and told her about someone shooting at me in the woods.

"Well, I didn't imagine the tent on my property." I was upset with the way she brushed off my concern.

"Look, Sam, people from around here are accustomed to using the land on this mountain for hunting, snowmobiling, fishing, hiking, all kinds of outdoor activities. And guess what—they go camping. You can't just come in and change the rules."

"What rules? Where does it say that I have to let anyone who pleases walk onto my private property? I'm telling you, Jean, someone shot at me."

"Did they hit you?"

"Of course not. I'm holding the phone talking to you, aren't I?"

"If someone shot at you and meant to hit you, they would have. You can count on that." I heard her ring up the cash register and shut the till drawer. "It was probably an errant shot from someone who was hunting squirrels or target shooting. I wouldn't get all worked up over it."

I slammed the phone down, feeling angrier than ever. Why wouldn't Jean take me seriously? I tried to think of what to do next. Should I report the trespasser and the shooting to the local authorities? I didn't even know whom to call; Clayton didn't have a town cop. I'd have to contact the county police, and I had a feeling they'd treat the matter in the same way Jean had—as if I were overreacting.

I was still fuming when Bernice brought Timmy home for supper. Timmy was splattered with mud from head to toe, but he wore a grin from ear to ear. "Aunt Sam, I caught a fish."

"A chub," Bernice said, as he jumped down from the four-wheeler. It's nothing you'd want to eat—too bony." I was relieved to hear that. I didn't have any intention of cleaning and cooking any fish. "But he did a good job reeling it in," she added, as she tousled Timmy's hair.

After Bernice left, I made Timmy take a long shower while I fixed us a supper of potato salad, lettuce wedges, tomatoes, and hard-boiled eggs.

"I bet Cody and Jason are eating fish for supper," Timmy complained. "Bernice and Cody caught some brook trout, and Bernice said she's gonna fry them in cornmeal. Jason got chubs, like me, and had to throw them back." He pushed his plate away.

"I bet trout taste good."

I made him eat half of what was on his plate, then I sent him outdoors to play with his trucks while I phoned Kate. I needed to talk to her.

Kate and I sat outside my cabin in lawn chairs while Timmy pushed his bulldozer around, filling it with sand, then emptying it into piles he smoothed to make roads for his Matchbox cars. I explained to Kate all the strange things that had been happening: the torn-down *No Hunting* signs, the threatening note on my door, the skinned raccoon, the blue tent on my land.

"Do you think all those things are connected?"

"I'm not sure," I said. "You know, another strange thing happened. This camper, whoever he is, was holding something in his hand, but I was too far away to make out what it was. He put it into a trunk and locked the lid. I wonder if that's significant."

"This whole thing gets weirder by the moment."

"I know. But I can't figure out what he wants. If it's just because I posted my land, there are better—saner—ways of getting me to change my mind."

Timmy hollered for our attention. I nodded to him as he pointed to the maze of little roads he'd created. Kate called out to him, "You'll be a construction boss when you grow up."

I told her then about the shooting and how the bullet had gone over my head. I told her, too, about Jean's reaction.

"Are you sure Jean's right—that it wasn't meant for you?"

"Let's hope she's right."

"Do you feel unsafe?" she asked, a worried look in her gray eyes.

"I'm not so concerned about me. But I don't like the idea of shooting going on with Timmy around. Even if it's just someone shooting at squirrels or whatever, what if he gets in the path of a stray bullet?"

Kate laid her hand on my shoulder. "Are you okay?"

I nodded. Just then Timmy interrupted us to play a game of badminton. He and Kate took me on and they won easily.

After the game, we moved inside. Timmy went reluctantly to

bed, and Kate and I sat on the futon couch while we talked over iced tea. She filled me in on the progress of her writing project, and since we were talking about work, I asked if she would have time to pose for me sometime. To my delight, she agreed.

"That's great." I couldn't imagine anyone I'd rather have sit for me.

"Do you give hugs to your models?" she asked, holding her arms out to me. I fell into her embrace, and she draped her arms around me, her fingers stroking the nape of my neck. Leaning into her, I felt the heat of her skin through her cotton shirt. Being so close to her made me feel weak and dizzy. I planted kisses on her throat as she wove her fingers in my hair. We were both aware that Timmy was in the room down the hall and maybe still awake. Finally, Kate pulled back, though she seemed reluctant when she said she had to go home.

When she stood to leave, she said again, "Are you sure you're not in danger here?"

I acted braver than I felt. "Someone's probably just trying to frighten me. I don't know who, but I'm going to find out. And I'm not going to let him scare me away."

"Just be careful," she said, stroking my face. I wanted her to stay, wanted to keep feeling her tender touch on my cheekbones.

After Kate drove off, I locked the door and closed all the drapes. Still, I kept listening for noises outside. Unable to settle down, I stayed up long past midnight. In my mind, I kept hearing the sharp report of a rifle, the parting of air by the force of a bullet.

When I finally got to sleep, a booming sound made me jump awake, my hand on my heart. Other muffled explosions followed, until slowly I realized that fireworks were going off in the distance. Probably some tourists setting off Roman candles somewhere on the mountain, even though it was illegal. The blasts and booms sounded just like gunshot, and the sounds seemed to go on forever. I had to wrap a pillow around my ears to muffle the noise. All night, dreams of being chased by someone with a gun kept me tossing and turning.

Chapter 13

A few weeks passed while I worked on the new series of paintings. Many days, Kate posed for me in the early mornings while the light was good, and I was getting a lot of work done on the painting of her in the wicker chair. It was glorious to have her sitting in front of me while I tried to capture her fine features. And we stole kisses once in a while.

Most days, Timmy played outdoors with his trucks while we worked, but he complained a lot. Jason and Cody had gone back to their parents' house in Clayton, and he missed them. "I'm bored, Aunt Sam," he whined constantly. Distracted by my work, I mostly ignored him.

One morning, he came into the studio and asked Kate to play Monopoly with him. "Kate's here so I can paint her," I said. "You go back downstairs and find something to do by yourself while we're working."

"We'll play another time, Timmy," Kate said. "Right now your aunt needs me to sit here and be still."

Timmy threw a black look at me before he clumped his way down the stairs, making a lot of noise on each step. For several hours, I painted furiously, and the morning sped by without my giving much thought to him.

Our arrangement was that Kate would pose until 11:00 a.m., have something to eat with me, then go back to her cottage to write. Usually, Timmy joined us for brunch, then grumbled that he hated soy sausages and wanted bacon. That day, while I was at the stove flipping an omelet with asparagus and artichoke, I called to him. He didn't come, so we went ahead and ate without him, lingering over chamomile tea. I expected that as soon as Kate left, he'd be underfoot and bellyaching about having nothing to do.

Kate helped me clear off the table and wash up the dishes before she left. From the door, she called "Goodbye, Timmy." I was surprised that he didn't at least come to see her off, as fond as he was of her. *He must be sulking in his bedroom.* But when I stepped in, the room was empty. The stuffed dog Jean had given him was on his unmade bed, and the Tonka trucks from Kate were lined up along the wall.

Timmy wasn't anywhere on the first floor. As I stood in the living area near the stone fireplace, trying to decide where to look next, a noise above my head made me jump. It sounded as if several tubes of paint or a can of brushes had been knocked off my worktable. Then it got abnormally quiet. "Timmy?" I called, but he didn't answer, so I walked upstairs to my studio, looking for him.

The first thing I saw was the painting I'd been working on. The easel was tipped over, and the painting of Kate in the wicker chair lay askew on the floor. I sank to my knees and touched the edges of the canvas, straightening it. I felt more than heard the gasp that tore from my mouth. Tears surfaced quickly and spilled onto the paint-smeared canvas. It was grotesque, what Timmy had done to it. Ruined. The picture had been scratched with paint directly from a tube. Thick, wavy lines of cadmium red bore gouges where the metal rim had dug into the canvas. The tube itself was lying on the edge of the worktable, crumbled and leaking paint like blood.

My perfect world, my sanctuary, had been invaded. Everything I held dear had changed abruptly and unexpectedly. I felt my cheeks grow hot with anger. Swiping at my tears with the back of my hand, I searched for the culprit. He was hiding behind a stack of canvases that I was going to ship out. I could see his blond hair and the rise of his back as he sat hunched behind the paintings. "Timmy!" I shrieked. "What in the world have you been doing? Just look at the mess you've made." I grabbed the nape of his shirt and dragged him out, knocking over two of the canvases that clattered to the floor. "Who said you could come up here by yourself?"

His shirt, arms, legs, face—all were marked with splotches

of red paint. When he looked up at me, his eyes were big and frightened, but I didn't even care. "Don't ever come up here again! This is my private place. This is where I work."

"I was just playing with the paint, Aunt Sam," he squeaked, his eyes darting wildly.

"Look at it—it's ruined!"

"No, it's not. I made it pretty. I was helping with your picture of Kate."

"Kids are not allowed here. Don't you get it? You can't come into my studio." I still had hold of his shirt, and I yanked on it. "Do you understand?"

He nodded, and I let go of the shirt. "Go," I said. "Go!"

"Where?" he asked, frantically tugging his shirt into place.

"Anywhere, I don't care. Just get out of here and leave me alone." After he left, I stared at the devastation of my studio.

I would get it back. With the frenzy of a madwoman, I straightened the studio, trying to reclaim it. Wiping the floor with a cloth soaked in mineral spirits, I erased marks of red paint from the pine boards. I stacked the finished canvases that Timmy had knocked over, tossed crumpled tubes of paint into the trash, and set the easel back on its feet. When I bent down to pick up the painting, I felt weak in the knees. I couldn't even look at it, marred with those ugly marks. I kicked it with my foot, sending the canvas skittering across the room. It rammed into the baseboard under the large, plate-glass window. I stared at the painting that had taken so much of my time, now lying at a useless angle on the floor.

I sat on the floor and looked out the window. The low-lying mountain range was green and blue and purple in the midday light. But all I saw was red. It took concentrating on my breathing, slowly marking the inhale and exhale of each breath, before I could calm down.

More relaxed now with my studio back to normal, I could think rationally. What had I done, sending Timmy away? What if he'd taken my words literally and left the cabin? In a state of panic, I ran down the stairs to look for him.

It made sense that Timmy would be in his room, consoling himself, huddled in his bed. But only the stuffed dog was there, lying carelessly on the floor as if it had been kicked aside. Socks and underwear spilled out the half-open drawers of the yellow dresser. Looking around the room, I realized that Timmy's red backpack was missing. I began to panic. What had I done? I tried to recall what I'd said to him in the heat of my anger. *Go away*, I'd said. Had he really thought I meant for him to leave?

Glancing at my watch, I saw that he hadn't been gone long. With any luck, I'd find him soon. After a quick search of the cabin, I went out to the yard. "Timmy? Timmy, come here!" I called. He wasn't under the steps or in the Jeep or behind the cabin near the emergency generator. Where could he be?

The shed door groaned when I pulled it open. Inside was stacked wood, the push lawnmower, a red can of gas, rakes, a garden spade, clipping shears, the few signs we hadn't hung yet. But Timmy was not hiding in the shed.

I ran over to Jean's house in case Timmy had gone over there. Jean wasn't home, but Badger was sleeping on the front porch. Lifting his head, he barked a few times. "It's just me, old boy," I said, pushing his water bowl closer to his nose. He lapped at the water while I got down on my hands and knees to look under the porch for Timmy. There wasn't a sign of him.

Rushing back toward my place along the lane, I called out his name. "Timmy, where are you? Come on out now. I'm not mad at you anymore." No answer, just the sound of deerflies buzzing. Winded, I stood in front of my cabin, my hands on my hips, and tried to think rationally. Where would a small boy go—a boy unfamiliar with the mountain? Timmy, in fact, was used to street signs and traffic lights and crosswalks. He'd easily get lost up here in the wilderness. He could be anywhere on the mountain, wandering in the woods.

I walked down the lane, scanning the woods on each side and shouting his name. Eventually, I came to the end of the lane where it butted up against the gravel road. At the opening of the stone fence, something red was lying near one of the granite posts. I bent down to discover it was a piece of Lego. Had it fallen from Timmy's backpack? Had he walked out this far?

On the other side of the road, Bernice was staining the

cedar shingles of her cabin. "Bernice," I called, "have you seen Timmy?"

At the sound of my voice, she looked up. She motioned *just a minute* with her index finger, set the paintbrush on the can of stain, then walked over to meet me in the center of the road. "What's up?"

"Timmy's wandered off. Have you seen him? He's probably carrying a backpack."

Bernice lifted the oversized sunglasses from her face. She looked at me carefully. "There hasn't been anyone around that I know of."

"So you didn't see him?"

"Did he run off? He shouldn't be roaming these woods by himself."

"If you do spot him, bring him over to my place, will you?" I headed back down my lane. "Please watch for him!" I called over my shoulder. I ran down the lane toward my cabin, then jumped into my Jeep, and drove out toward the gravel road. By then, Bernice was putting the cover on the can of stain.

With the Jeep idling between the granite posts, I sat with my hands on the steering wheel. Which way would Timmy have gone? To the left farther up Hurricane Mountain? Or to the right down the mountain? Which way would I go if I were an eight-year-old boy? Toward home, of course, or the direction most likely to lead home. I turned right and headed down the mountain.

Driving slowly, I stopped every few feet to peer into the denser woods on either side of the gravel road. I kept my eyes ahead, too, hoping to spot him trudging along the road. I pictured his little body, his blond head bent, the pack strapped onto his back.

The thought of the stranger who had been camping in the woods crossed my mind. His tent was quite a distance from here, over on the back side of my property, but still if there was some lunatic wandering the woods, Timmy could be in even greater danger.

Now I was really panicked. As the Jeep inched along the road, I yelled until my throat was sore. "Timmy, come on now! Aunt Sam's looking for you. Take a ride in the Jeep with me. We'll go to McDonald's in Fredericksville. We can go shopping. Timmy!"

I never knew the mountain could be so quiet. As I scanned the woods, my ears were peeled for the sound of footsteps crunching pine needles and decayed leaves, twigs snapping, branches swaying. But everything was still.

I snapped my head at a movement out of the corner of my eye, but it was just a rabbit. A chipmunk darted down the embankment and disappeared. A few sparrows flitted from bush to bush.

I continued moving at a crawl, tooting the horn and shouting Timmy's name. Crossing the small wooden bridge over the brook, I felt the boards sag under the Jeep's weight. I slipped the gears into neutral in the middle of the bridge and searched out the driver's side window, eyeing the brook that cascaded down from underground springs higher on the mountain. Nothing there, just leaves and pieces of deadwood swirling on the water. Shifting in my seat, I cast my eyes out the passenger window. The brook on that side made a sharp bend, cutting into the bank, and I couldn't see very far. I was about to drive on, but then it occurred to me that Timmy might be hiding under the bridge. I put the Jeep into gear and moved off the bridge, then pulled to the side of the road. I scurried down toward the brook, nearly slipping on the steep embankment.

There was a spot between the bridge supports and the water that was dry and sheltered. I knew it from fishing for trout. I crawled under the bridge, wiping the fine strands of a spider web from my face. Indications someone had been here recently were everywhere. The soft soil was indented with footsteps and handprints. Stooping, I investigated more closely. Yes, they were the prints of a child. My heart started to skip in my chest. He'd been here!

I inched backward from under the bridge and stood to see where the footprints led. I followed them downstream, picking my way along the bank, pushing back alder bushes and stepping over tree roots. When I approached the sharp bend in the brook, I had to hold onto tree limbs to navigate my way. My head was down, watching my footing, and when I made it around the bend, I raised my head and saw Timmy's red backpack. It was lying in the damp sand, part of it sticking into the water. One broken black strap swayed on the water's surface.

I hurried over to the backpack and picked it up, grabbing it to my chest. Water dripped onto my shirt and jeans. I was on the right track, here was evidence of that. But I still hadn't found Timmy. Quickly, I tossed the backpack onto higher ground. Then I knelt and laid my hand over a footprint that was the size of Timmy's sneaker. Lifting my hand, I turned it over and stared at the wet sand and little bits of stone clinging to it. Timmy must have been here, but what did it mean that his footprints led to the water and ended? Terrible images of him floating facedown, bobbing among the rocks, flashed through my mind.

I had to think clearly. Thrusting both hands into the brook, I tossed cold water onto my face. *You've got to keep walking, Sam,* I told myself. So I pushed on, searching the banks and brook for any sign of Timmy. The heat was prickly, and I had to wipe my forehead with the back of my hand to keep sweat out of my eyes.

Out of the stillness, the sound of a motorized vehicle came crashing though the woods. The sound grew near, and soon Bernice came roaring between the trees on her four-wheeler.

I waved and hollered until she spotted me. She maneuvered the four-wheeler over to where I was standing and quieted the motor. "When I saw you squeal out of your place, I thought you must be really worried," she said, still straddling the machine. "Did you find anything yet?"

"Timmy's backpack. His footprints leading into the brook. But then I lost the trail. I'm getting frantic. He doesn't know his way around the woods. Anything could happen to him."

"We'll find him," Bernice said. "He'll be fine." But I detected a note of uneasiness in her voice. "Why don't you go back to your Jeep and phone for help? I'll keep looking along here."

"I don't want to leave. What if we find Timmy and he needs me?"

"I know these woods better than you, and I can cover more ground on this." She patted the machine.

I hesitated, wiping the sweat from my brow again. "I don't know."

119

"We need more searchers, Samantha. We want to find him before dark."

The thought of Timmy spending the night alone in the woods terrified me. "All right. I'll phone Kate and Jean."

"Jean will know folks she can call, too." Bernice started revving the motor. "I'm going to follow along the brook," she said as she crept away on the four-wheeler, peering into the tall brush that cluttered the bank.

I ran back toward the road, enduring the snap-back of branches in my face. When I reached the Jeep, I tried calling Kate on my cell phone, but it couldn't pick up a signal. *Out of service area* read the letters on the tiny screen. Tossing the phone onto the front seat, I put the Jeep in gear and tore off up the mountain, hoping a higher altitude would allow better reception.

Stopping on the road just near the turnoff to my place, I tried again. Still no reception. Frustrated, I threw the phone onto the seat and sped down the lane to my cabin. I ran into the kitchen and dialed Kate's number on the portable phone. This time, it rang through. When I heard her voice on the other end, I almost broke down, but I knew I didn't have time for tears or hysteria. "Kate," I said, steadying my voice, "Timmy's lost. He ran away and wandered off into the woods, and I can't find him." I was speaking so fast my words ran into each other. "Please come," I gulped.

"I'll be there as soon as I can. Stay calm," she said, and her soft voice quieted my heart a little.

"Come to the bridge by the brook. Bernice's looking for him there."

As soon as I hung up, I called The Village Store. When Robby answered, I yelled for him to put Jean on. The receiver made a clunk as it dropped onto the counter, then Jean picked it up and her voice came over the line.

"Timmy's missing," I cried. "He ran off into the woods. Bernice's looking for him on the four-wheeler."

"I'm on my way," Jean said. "Where should I meet you?"

"At the bridge by the trout brook," I said, out of breath. "If I'm not there, just start looking for him. His footprints led to the

120

west and followed along the brook until I lost them."

"All right. You go back to the bridge. I'll be there as soon as I can." Jean seemed ready to hang up, then she added, "Are you calling from home?"

"Yeah."

"Before you leave, grab something of Timmy's that's got his smell on it. A shirt or something. I left Badger home today—go get him. He knows Timmy's scent."

"Jean, bring help."

"There's a few guys here in the store I can ask. I'll have Robby make some phone calls."

I didn't even bother to say goodbye. I dropped the phone into its cradle and quickly grabbed a dirty T-shirt of Timmy's that was lying on the floor beside his bed, then hurried out the door with it in my fist.

As I pulled into the driveway of Jean's cabin, Badger jumped up from the porch and began barking and straining at his chain. "Hey, old boy," I undid his chain, "you're coming with me." He jumped into the Jeep when I patted the seat, and we hurried down the mountain, Badger's head out the window with his tongue lolling.

Just before the bridge, I parked off the road and hooked Badger's leash to his collar. "You're going to help me find Timmy," I told him as he leaped down from the seat. I held out Timmy's T-shirt for him to smell, then led him down the bank. Under the bridge, I had Badger sniff the shirt again, then Timmy's footprint in the mud. We took off into the woods, Badger sniffing the ground along the brook and pulling me along with him.

We walked a long way, following a path Bernice had carved with the four-wheeler. Badger kept sniffing the ground, so I figured we must all be on the right trail. At a place where the brook snaked around a clump of trees, Badger broke from Bernice's path and strained toward a rise in the woods. I let him lead me on. When we reached the top of the rise and came out of a thick grove of balsam trees, I could see a small clearing—a wild meadow—farther down the mountain. Badger yanked at his leash and pulled me off in that direction.

He began jumping wildly around my feet, and I knelt to pat him and quiet him. Then I got out my binoculars to see what had him so riled up. A black bear was at the edge of the meadow, moving on all fours toward a patch of blackberry bushes. After I adjusted the focus, I could see the fur on its haunches rippling as its paws hit the ground. I didn't want Badger exciting the bear, so I untied the neckerchief from around my neck and wrapped it around his snout. "It's okay, boy. We've got to stay quiet." I pushed gently on his rump to make him sit. Jean had trained him well. His ears were bent back against his head and he pawed the ground, but he kept quiet, whimpering softly.

I lifted the binoculars again and saw that the bear had moved closer to the patch of blackberries. Swinging my head, I saw something else through the lenses. Timmy! He was picking berries, plucking each black jewel from the bush and stuffing it into his mouth. He seemed oblivious to the bear. I wanted to scream out a warning to him, but then I saw Bernice behind Timmy. She'd spotted me and was making an emphatic tamping-down motion with her hands, cautioning me to be silent. I had to trust her; she knew more about these woods, more about the habits of bears, than I would ever know.

I tied Badger's leash to the trunk of a birch tree. Bent over and hunched down, I sneaked closer until I was within a few yards of Bernice. Timmy was unaware of Bernice and intent on picking and eating blackberries. He'd had only a piece of toast and a small glass of apple juice for breakfast and no lunch.

Suddenly, the bear snarled and reared up, towering over the bush, facing Timmy. Startled, Timmy dropped his handful of berries, spilling them on the ground. He made like he was going to run, but Bernice crept up behind him and stopped him. "Don't startle it," I heard her say. "Just back away. No sudden movement. If you stay quiet, you'll be okay." Placing her hands on Timmy's shoulders, she guided him backward, stepping very slowly. My heart was thumping in my chest as I watched, and I did everything I could to keep from running over and grabbing Timmy. But I had to trust Bernice.

Hovering over them, the bear growled, shaking its paws and

extending the claws. Its eyes were small, its nose long, its ears rounded. Its incisor teeth were pointed and looked like they could tear a gash in someone's neck. Strings of drool dripped from its mouth as the bear batted at them. Timmy seemed to go limp, but Bernice caught him under the arms. "Stand up and stay close to me," she said. "If we move away slowly, it'll move away, too." She pulled Timmy along with her, shuffling backward. I thought the bear was going to lunge at them. The muscles of its shoulders rippled. Then it roared once more and dropped to all fours. For what seemed like a long time, it just stood there, its beady eyes staring at them. I could do nothing but watch from my vantage point, my heart bursting out of my ribcage. I was afraid to breathe. Finally, slowly, the bear turned and lumbered off into the woods, looking back, sniffing the air, moving on.

I saw Timmy slump back against Bernice, and I heard Bernice say, "I told you it would be okay. Any time you meet up with a bear, don't run. A black bear won't usually tangle with a human, but it will chase something that moves quickly. If you back away, it'll usually back away, too." Bernice placed her hands on Timmy's shoulders and turned him so that they were facing each other. "You did the right thing," she told him. "That bear didn't want you, it just wanted your berries." Timmy nodded solemnly. His face was pale, smeared with blackberry juice and dirt. His arms and neck were bitten up by mosquitoes, making ugly red welts on his skin. There were scratches on his hands and a rip in the knee of his jeans.

Looking past Bernice, he spotted me. I held my arms out and it seemed he was going to run to me, but then he held himself back. "You were courageous, Timmy," I said, coming closer to him. "I'm proud of you." He stuck his hands in his pockets, trying to look brave. Watching him, really seeing him, perhaps for the first time, I thought, *a small boy shouldn't have to always put a brave face to the world. A boy needs a place where he feels safe and loved and protected.* I reached out to him, and he fell into my arms, sobbing. It seemed natural to hold him. Like a mother, I wanted to shield him. I took Timmy's hand and led him over to where Badger was tied up. He sank to his knees and untied the neckerchief, and Badger let out a happy bark, licking his face. Timmy buried his head in the dog's neck, and the tears came hard, wrenching from his tiny body. It was the first time since his parents died that he had really cried.

When Timmy had exhausted himself with crying, Bernice helped him onto the backseat of the four-wheeler. "I'm going to get you home now," she said. Timmy hugged her back as Bernice turned the key and the engine choked to life. Badger and I followed them to the road. The dog was barking excitedly now, and I let him. Timmy kept looking back at us, but he never let go of his grip on Bernice. Bernice had a shrill whistle she blew every few minutes to let the others know we were coming.

A half hour later when we got to the road, I was surprised at the crowd that had gathered. Jean was there, of course, and Badger ran right to her, gobbling up the treat she held out to him. Several men I recognized as store customers milled about, including Robby's dad and Bernice's son-in-law. Another group of men and women in orange hunting vests leaned against dusty cars and trucks lined up along the edge of the road. Kate had a gallon thermos of something cold—ice water or lemonade—that she was doling out in paper cups. Bernice helped Timmy climb down from the four-wheeler, and he stood with his head down, bashful and dirty.

Kate was the first to go to him. She knelt down and wrapped her arms around him, not caring that his face was smeared with snot and blackberry juice. She held him and kind of rocked him, then everyone circled around them, patting Timmy on the head or the shoulder and murmuring, "Glad you're okay." "We were worried about you." "Quite a little trek, huh?"

Bernice stepped in to rescue him from the crowd. "Timmy," she said, "tell them about the bear."

Kate released Timmy from her hug and stood up. "What bear?" she asked, looking down at him.

Timmy shyly looked at her, then from face to face, and I didn't think he would talk. But then he said, "A big one! And it was coming right at me!" Like a seasoned Maine storyteller, he rattled off the tale of his adventure in the woods and his encounter with the bear.

As I scanned the faces in the crowd, I saw one that made me stop and look again. Garret Belling stood on the edges of the group of searchers and well-wishers. His eyes met mine with such intensity that I turned my gaze away. When I looked back, he had disappeared.

Chapter 14

That evening, I asked Jean to bring home a pound of hamburger and some buns from the store, and she dropped them off for me. I could tell she wanted to make some snide comment about my being a vegetarian, but she kept it to herself as she handed me the meat wrapped in butcher paper.

Though I gagged while forming the patty, I made a fat cheeseburger for Timmy's supper. I hadn't inquired why he'd run away. For now, I just wanted to make him feel safe again. We had a picnic of sorts, the two of us, sitting in front of the cabin on a blanket. "How would you like it if we got a TV up here?"

"Really?" His mouth was crammed full of cheeseburger and his chin was greasy, but his eyes lit up.

I nibbled at my sandwich of avocado and provolone cheese. "We can get satellite reception, I think. I'll look into it if you want."

"That'd be cool," he said, taking another big bite. "Maybe I can get my PlayStation from Grandma's house. And my video games."

"We'll ask her to mail them to you."

Following supper, Timmy soaked for a long time in the tub, playing with a plastic submarine. I knocked on the door and asked if he needed help washing his hair.

"Okay," he said.

I scrubbed his blond hair until it was frothy. He squinted his eyes shut while I poured warm water over his head with a plastic cup. I stepped out of the bathroom so he could towel off, and soon he walked out wearing boxers and a white T-shirt.

"These mosquito bites itch." He made to scratch the back of

his leg.

I grabbed his hand. "Don't scratch. That just makes them worse." I dabbed calamine lotion on his bites. "There, you're covered with pink polka dots. They won't itch much now with this lotion on them."

He climbed into bed, and I handed him the stuffed dog Jean had given him. This time, he took it and tucked it under his arm. "That was good that Badger didn't bark when the bear was scaring me, wasn't it?"

"He knew better than to make the bear nervous. Do you know that Badger led me right to you? That's how I found you. He followed your scent."

"Wow. Dogs are pretty smart. I'm going to get a dog someday. One just like Badger."

"Jean said you can play with Badger whenever you want." I pulled the sheet and blanket up over his legs. "Now what if I read you a bedtime story before we turn out the light?"

He looked away, pulling threads on the top of the stuffed dog's head. "I guess."

"What have we got here that we can read?" I thought of my bookshelves in the other room, crowded with books about art. I didn't have a single children's book in the cabin.

Timmy smoothed the dog's head with his hand. "You could just tell me a story."

"Okay." So I sat on the edge of his bed and told him a story about Dan as a young boy. "I got lost one time, too. Dan and I were at the mall in Warwick with our mother."

"Grandma?"

"Right. Your father was supposed to stay with me while Grandma went into the bank to cash a check. We were to wait in the hall outside the bank door, and Dan wasn't supposed to let go of my hand. He was older than me, you know, and his job was always to look after me."

"What happened?"

"I did something I shouldn't have done. I pulled away from Dan and ran down the hall because I saw a girl I thought I knew from our neighborhood. She was wearing pink sneakers, and I wanted to ask her where she got them."

Timmy made a face. "Pink shoes."

"I know. But I thought they were pretty special back then. I ran all the way after her, chasing her down the mall. She went around a corner, and I followed her. But when I finally caught up with her, it wasn't the girl from our neighborhood at all. And then when I turned around to find Dan, he was gone. I didn't know where I was, and I couldn't see my mother anywhere, either."

"Were you scared?"

"You bet. I sat right down on the floor by the wall and cried, but I didn't want anybody to see me crying so I faced the wall with my back to the crowd. And I had to go to the bathroom, and that worried me too because I was afraid I'd pee my pants."

"How did you get found, Aunt Sam?"

"Your father found me. I felt someone tapping my shoulder, and I turned around and it was Dan. He held out his hand and I grabbed it and he led me back to the door outside the bank. And you know what? He never told Grandma that I'd run away."

"So he was like a hero?"

"Sort of."

Timmy was adamant. "Yeah, he was. He was a hero, just like Badger was a hero to find me."

The sky was ebony, clear of any cloud cover, when I sat again on the blanket spread over the grass. Timmy was sleeping soundly inside the cabin. Hugging my knees, I thought about the day's events. I hadn't realized how frightened and worried I'd been while Timmy was missing and how relieved when he was found. It felt right to have him home again, safe in his room, in his own bed. *His room. His bed.* When had I begun to think of it that way?

Here it was August already. School would be starting in less than a month. We had some big decisions to make—Timmy and I. It didn't look like Uncle Bill and Aunt Millie were going to work out as a home for him. My cousin Chris had recovered and moved back to Boston, but Uncle Bill and Aunt Millie were exhausted from caring for her and were off on an Alaskan cruise to rest.

They hadn't renewed their offer to take Timmy. And, of course, my mother wasn't up to caring for a young boy. I was worried about her health; she seemed to have gone downhill since Dan's death. In our phone conversations, I'd been encouraging her to move in with her sister Charlotte. If my mother did that, she'd sell her house.

The options for Timmy were narrowing.

A movement in the sky caught the corner of my eye, and I looked up. A shooting star sped across the sky, then disappeared. Lying back, my head in the pillow of my arms, I thought of the story I'd told Timmy. I hadn't recalled that incident for years. Now I remembered Dan taking my hand, could almost feel him pulling me to my feet. He'd used his handkerchief to wipe my face, and when he saw the way I was standing with my legs crossed, he'd waited outside the women's restroom for me. Taking my hand again, he'd led me back to the bank. When our mother came out, she didn't even know I'd been gone.

Another shooting star broke away and raced across the sky, trailing a hint of green. I realized it must be the Perseid meteorite showers. More meteorites zipped by, crisscrossing the sky, and soon it began to look like fireworks overhead.

I went inside and tried to wake Timmy. He was curled up in his bed, still hugging the stuffed dog. Nudging his shoulder, I said, "Timmy, come see this!" He groaned and rolled over in bed, his back to me. Impulsively, I scooped him up in my arms, and the dog fell to the floor. He was heavy when I carried him outside, letting the screen door slam behind us. He stirred at the sound but didn't wake. Carefully, I laid him down on the blanket. "Timmy," I said, "wake up and look at the sky."

He opened one eye. "Aunt Sam?" he mumbled.

I shook his shoulders gently. "Wake up, Timmy. This only happens once a year. You don't want to miss it."

"I'm cold," he whimpered.

I wrapped the blanket around his legs. "Come awake now. Watch the shooting stars with me."

He grumbled, but his eyes opened.

"Look up there." I took his hand and pointed to the sky. "Keep your eyes on the sky, and you'll see stars moving fast like they're falling."

"Are they going to hurt us?"

"No. It's just pieces of meteors and other stuff in the sky far, far away. But see how pretty it is."

"I see one," he yelled, coming into a sitting position. "Right there."

He was wide awake now. We watched for twenty minutes or longer, both of us exclaiming over the spectacular celestial show. The action slowed down after a while, and it was then that I said, "Timmy, why did you run away today?"

He pulled the blanket tighter around his legs. "I don't know."

"Of course you do. Someone doesn't just run away for no reason at all. What was it?"

"I'm cold. I want to go back to bed."

I put my arm around his shoulder and pulled him into my body heat. "You tell me first, then we'll go inside."

He pushed away from me. "You didn't want me here. You were mad at me."

"I was mad about the mess you made in my studio, but that doesn't mean I don't want you here. What makes you think I don't want you around?"

"You act like I'm in the way, just somebody you got to take care of."

"Is that what you think?"

"You know it's true!" he cried. "You don't want me, and I don't want to be here neither."

He's right. Timmy had been with me for nearly two months, and in all that time, I hadn't made a place for him in my heart. He'd been an intruder, a pest who got in the way of my work, someone who needed looking after when I didn't want to look after anyone except myself.

He was crying now. "I want to go home and see my mom and dad. I want everything to be the way it used to be."

"That's not possible. You know that." Again I tried to hug him, and again he pushed me away. I was frustrated at my inability to reach him. "Why don't you go back to bed for now?" I said softly. "We'll talk about this some more tomorrow."

He jumped up and, trailing the blanket, ran into the house.

Timmy was quiet and withdrawn the next day, but that changed when Jason and Cody came over to play in the afternoon. They said their grandma had driven down to their parents' house in Clayton and brought them up to see Timmy. I couldn't very well tell them they weren't welcome, that I had work to do, but I did tell the boys they had to play outside. I attempted to work in my studio, cleaning up the mess, restoring the canvas of Kate that Timmy had damaged, but I could hear the boys hooting and hollering as they pushed each other on the swing. I was about to give up trying to get any work done and was putting my brushes away when I heard rapping on the front door.

Bernice was standing on the front step. "I want you to go for a ride with me." She waved her hand toward her parked four-wheeler, the plastic tortoise bracelets on her wrist jangling.

I opened the screen door and stepped out. "I can't just leave Timmy here alone."

"Jason will watch him. He's pretty responsible. He's used to looking after Cody."

After what Bernice had done the day before to find Timmy, I couldn't refuse. We told the boys we'd be back shortly and we drove off, Bernice in front steering and me behind, holding onto the rack at the side of my seat. The heavy aroma of her lilac perfume drifted back to me. I was curious about where she was taking me, but we couldn't really talk over the sound of the motor.

Bernice turned onto the logging road and drove us down over a long slope. She pulled to a stop in front of the blue tent.

"Is that damn thing still here?" I fumed as I dismounted.

Bernice shut off the motor. "I got to thinking about what you'd told me, so I came down here this morning to see for myself. Someone's camping here all right."

"Any idea who it is?"

"I have an idea."

"Well, spit it out."

Instead of answering, Bernice climbed off the four-wheeler and walked over to the tent. She unzipped the flap and peered inside. I could see over her shoulder that the tent was still well stocked with canned foods, bottled water, toiletries, reading material, battery lamps, and a duffel bag of clothing. A black hooded sweatshirt hung on the middle post, and the sleeping bag looked like it had been slept in recently.

"So who is it, Bernice? Can't you just level with me?"

She let the flap door fall closed. "Did you see Garret Belling yesterday when we brought Timmy out of the woods?"

"Yes. I wondered what he was doing there."

"So did I. As far as I knew, he was supposed to be on vacation. The word around the mill was that he'd told everyone he was going to be in Hawaii or Cancun or someplace like that. So what was he doing up here? It just didn't make sense. I started putting two and two together."

"And?"

Bernice walked around to the side of the tent where the metal footlocker sat. "He's been telling my son-in-law Harry he wants to buy a place where he can fish and hunt. But, you know, I think it's something else. I could tell that right away that day when we were at the trout brook. He's good at fishing, knows what he's doing, but he didn't seem interested in it. Seemed like something else was on his mind, like fishing was just an excuse to get me up here and grill me about the area."

"You think Garret is camping out here. But why?"

Bernice reached behind the footlocker and lifted up a fishing rod that was lying on the ground. "Look at this. Here's his pole, and it's still got a worm on the hook." She flicked at the dried-up worm with her index finger. "That guy doesn't take care of his equipment. It's not fishing he's interested in." Bernice cleaned off the hook and neatly caught it onto the reel. I watched her place the pole against the tent.

"What is it he wants then?"

"I don't know. When he was up here that day, he went on and on about how he wanted to buy some land on the mountain, put up a cabin like mine so he could fish and hunt whenever he wanted.

He'd been drinking, so I wrote off what he said as just the beer talking."

"I thought you two were friends."

With the toe of her sequined sneaker, Bernice nudged the side of the footlocker. "What gave you that idea? I hardly know him."

"But don't you work together?"

"We both work at the mill, but that's as far as it goes. I'm in the office, and Garret's out on the floor on the rewinding machine. My son-in-law Harry sees him most days, but I only run into him once in a while. I was surprised when he started coming into the office to talk to me. At first, he just made small talk about work, but then he began asking about Hurricane Mountain and asking me to bring him up here fishing."

Bernice knelt down and fingered the lock on the latch. She let go of it, and it clanked as it hit the side of the metal trunk. "What the hell is in this anyhow?"

"Locked pretty tight, isn't it?"

"I can fix that in a hurry." Bernice lifted bolt cutters out of a toolbox on the back of the four-wheeler. She was continuously surprising me with her ingenuity and know-how. "You hold that padlock away from the trunk so I can work on it."

I did what she asked. I was curious about what was locked up in the metal trunk and hopping mad that the trespasser on my property was probably Garret Belling.

It took both of us to cut through the lock. I don't know what I expected to see when Bernice opened the trunk. "Well, I'll be damned. This thing looks empty," she said. "Why would a guy bother to lock it if there's nothing in it?"

Leaning forward, I peered into the trunk. It was old and musty smelling, a relic from some war. I patted the sides and the bottom. "Wait a minute. There's something under here, I think." I lifted a false bottom and revealed a large folder.

"What have you got there?"

The folder was full of papers, which I rifled through. "Looks like blueprints or architectural drawings or something like that."

"Spread them out here and let's get a good look." Bernice pointed to a flat, grassy area next to the tent.

I took a handful and Bernice took a handful, and we laid them out on the ground. The papers seemed to be building plans of some sort. One was a surveyor's map of my property.

I poked the map with my index finger. "What's he doing with this?"

Bernice took the map, turning it around in her hands and scanning it. "That son of a bitch is serious." Bernice handed back the map and looked at me cautiously. "You should know that Garret's been asking all kinds of questions, like how much property you own. When we were fishing, he asked point blank if I thought you'd ever sell."

"Why is he so interested in my place? There's more land on the mountain if he really wants to buy. He doesn't need to go nosing around my property."

"Let's look at more of this stuff and see if we can figure it out."

Down on our hands and knees, we moved from document to document, unfolding each one and studying it. After a few minutes, Bernice found something. "Ski slopes."

"What's that?" I asked, looking up from a sheaf of paper.

"These are plans for ski slopes, all along this back end of your property."

I looked over her shoulder at the plans. "Is that what this is? Plans for a ski slope?"

"These hills would make a damn nice place to ski. In fact, it'd be the perfect place on the mountain for it."

I raised my head and looked at the terrain all around me, above and below. I saw rolling hills, steep hills, wide clearings among pine trees, bumps and drop-offs. "What does Garret think this is?" I said. "Surgarloaf? Sunday River?"

"Maybe that's what he's up to. I bet he plans to build a ski resort here. Of course, it'd have to be on a smaller scale than either Sugarloaf or Sunday River."

"I don't have enough land for ski slopes."

"Well, there's something else you don't know. There's talk around the mill that the lumber company is planning to sell all the acres it owns next to you. You put the two properties together, and you've got several hundred acres."

"Garret doesn't have money for that kind of operation, does he?"

"I wouldn't think so," Bernice agreed. "But he might think he can get the backing of someone who does. Knowing him, he's dreamed up some grandiose idea that if he nails down a good deal on the property, he can get financing from a developer."

"He can just forget those plans. There's no way he's getting his hands on my property."

We picked up the rest of the documents that were strewn on the ground and put them back in the trunk, although we were not neat about it and we did not put back the false bottom.

Bernice refolded a topographical map that showed the different elevations of the property, tossed it into the trunk, and let the lid drop down.

"Just a minute," I said, lifting the cover again. I found a pencil stub, and on the back of one of the pieces of paper, I scribbled, *We know what you're up to.* Then I slammed the lid down. "Okay. We can leave now."

When I climbed onto the four-wheeler behind Bernice, she said over her shoulder, "Be careful, Samantha. Garret's cunning and more clever than you think." Then she turned the key, and we rumbled up the long hill toward my cabin.

"I wonder what's the best step to take now," I said as I dismounted. We'd pulled to a stop in my yard, but Bernice remained seated with the motor idling.

She adjusted the bright orange visor on her head. "I'm going to stay at my cabin while this is going on," she said, "instead of going back to my house in Fredericksville. I can commute to the mill from here. I'll feel better being here to look after my place."

"Do you think Garret's dangerous?"

"I think he's desperate. My son-in-law Harry told me Garret got into some trouble at the mill, and his foreman is planning to let him go. They've given him two warnings already, so he knows he's apt to get sacked."

"Jean should know what's going on. I'll fill her in tonight

when she gets home from the store."

"Do you want me to sit in on the conversation?"

My first impulse was to say no, but then I reconsidered. Bernice knew Garret better than I did, and her perspective would be important. "Sure. Come over around 9:30, if that's not too late."

"I'll be here." She revved the engine. "Jason, Cody," she called, and the boys suddenly materialized.

"We were playing baseball in the field." Cody was out of breath, and he had a scratch on his knee. "You should've seen the hit I made, Grandma."

They must have run over to Bernice's cabin to get equipment while we were gone. Cody leaned on an aluminum bat, and Jason was tossing a baseball in the air and catching it. Timmy was wearing a catcher's mitt that was too big for him. Timmy's cheeks were red, and his clothes were rumpled. "I'm not very good at catching," he said.

Bernice said, "You play with these boys long enough, you'll learn." She looked at me. "Well, I should get back to my cabin. I've got to finish staining the shingles." Then she shifted into gear and called to her grandsons, "You boys come home in time for supper. And don't make pests of yourselves around here."

Bernice was prompt. She showed up at precisely 9:30 that night. I offered her something to drink. "I'll take a soda, if you have any."

I noticed a sheepish look on her face when I handed her a glass of ice cubes and a can of cola. Jean had told me that the gossip around the village was that Bernice had quit drinking and was attending AA meetings in Fredericksville.

"I'm keeping a close eye on my place these days," she said. "Who knows, maybe Garret's after the whole damn mountain. Greedy son of a bitch."

We moved into the living room and sat by the fire, Bernice in the pine rocker and me on the futon couch. Timmy was already dressed for bed, wearing pajama bottoms. He sat cross-legged on the floor, playing a game of solitaire.

"Is Jason and Cody here, too?" he asked when he spotted Bernice.

"Nope. Just me. The boys went back to their parents' house for the night."

"Why?"

"Because I have to go to work in the morning."

"Do you want to play cribbage?" Timmy asked. "Aunt Sam has been teaching me."

"I haven't played cribbage in years. Sometime I'll show you how to play penny poker, but not tonight," Bernice said. She smiled and asked, "Have you seen any bears lately?"

"I stay close to the cabin now," Timmy said.

"That's smart." Bernice leaned back in the rocker and crossed her legs, swinging one foot. "Did I tell you about the time I saw a bear cub up in a tree?"

Timmy was all ears. "Did it climb up there by itself?"

"Sure did. Bears are good tree climbers. I was hiking in the woods, and I saw this cub in a tree. Just hanging on and watching me. I knew the mama bear had to be nearby, and I didn't want to get between her and her cub."

"What'd you do?"

"I turned around, walked back out of the woods, and let them be. Just like when you walked away from that black bear. It's the best thing to do."

Timmy smiled at that.

We heard barking, then Jean knocking at the front door. She didn't wait for me to let her in, but just walked in and helped herself to a Miller Lite in the fridge. "We're in here," I called, and she joined us in the living room, sitting on the futon with me.

Badger made his way directly to Timmy and sniffed his legs. Timmy laughed and patted his head.

"Time for you to be in bed," I said.

"Can't I stay up? Everyone's here."

"It's not a party, Timmy. We're going to have a grown-up talk."

Jean reached over and tousled his hair. "You heard your aunt. Bedtime."

Timmy knelt on the floor and gave Badger a big hug and was rewarded with a wet kiss on the ear. Then he wandered off toward his bedroom, and Badger settled on the floor by Jean's feet.

"This is unexpected," she said, setting her can of beer on the pine-slab coffee table. "All the neighbors in one room and being civil to each other. What's up?"

"We think we've uncovered a plot to take over my land," I said.

"You aren't being paranoid again, are you? And now you've brought Bernice in on it, too?"

"It's a real concern, Jean," Bernice said, covetously eyeing the can of beer. She gripped the arms of the rocker and went on. "We found plans for building a ski slope right on this very spot."

"That's ridiculous. Who would invest in something like that up here?"

"We don't know, but we do think we know who's been gathering information." Bernice leaned back in the rocker.

"It's Garret," I said. "We found proof." We filled her in on our discovery of the trunk and the blueprints and maps.

Jean got up and went into the kitchen for another beer. As she was opening the can, she said, "He wouldn't have enough land to put in a ski slope with just Samantha's property." She tossed the flip-top onto the coffee table and sat back down on the futon.

"The lumber company is selling their acreage," Bernice said.

"That's news to me."

"Well, it's pretty hush-hush right now, but Garret must have found out that the land would be up for sale."

"Even with that land too, he'd have a small operation for a ski resort."

"Maybe he plans to get his hands on your land, too," I said. "After all, he could convince you it'd be good for business at the store if there were a lot of tourists here in the winter, as well as in the summer."

"Yeah, and maybe he thinks he can butter me up to sell because we both work at the mill," Bernice added. "He's probably going after Samantha first because she's new here and he thinks he can scare her away to get her property cheap."

"Well, if any of this is true, I'm still not convinced that Garret is serious about it," Jean said, "or that he has any real financial backing. It could just be a pipe dream, some stupid fantasy."

"Either way, I still think he could be dangerous," Bernice said. "He doesn't always act rationally." She related an incident at the mill when Garret had lost his temper because another worker was getting more overtime than he was. "He intentionally pushed him toward one of the big paper machines. The guy could have had his hand mangled if another worker nearby hadn't grabbed him and pulled him away from the machine." Bernice poured the rest of the cola into her glass of ice cubes. "Of course, Garret claimed it was an accident. Said he didn't push the guy, he fell into him."

"It does sound like he's a son of a bitch," Jean conceded. "But don't you think the three of us can handle him? Let's just confront him and make him tell us what he's up to."

"Do you think that's wise? To go face to face with Garret?" I asked.

"If the three of us face him together, it might have some impact," Bernice offered. "It would let him know that he's not going to make any headway with any one of us."

We agreed that we would talk to Garret, but we decided not to make any hasty moves. "Let's think it over and see if we can come up with a plan," I said. "We don't want to push him into a corner and make him do something violent."

Chapter 15

Even as I tried to come up with an idea of how to handle Garret, another matter pressed in on me. The time had come to make a decision about the school year. Since there didn't seem to be a way to send Timmy back to Rhode Island, I tossed around the idea of keeping him with me. But would the small village school at the foot of the mountain—kindergarten through grades six all in one building—be able to give Timmy the kind of education he deserved? What would my brother have thought about Timmy attending Clayton Elementary School? Well, I couldn't think about that. Timmy was here with me now, and I had to decide what was best for both of us.

Already Jason and Cody had begun talking about the new school year starting. The boys were around a lot more regularly now that Bernice, who had put her house in Fredericksville on the market, was staying at her cabin more and more often these days. Timmy loved having friends close by, and the three of them spent most waking hours together whenever the boys were staying with their grandmother.

"I'm getting new clothes," Jason bragged. They were sitting on my front stoop, taking a break from a sweaty game of flag football and drinking lemonade. I was hanging clothes on the line and overheard their conversation.

"Yeah, and all the school stuff, too," Cody piped in. "Pencils and markers and a ruler and crayons and all that stuff."

Jason downed his lemonade and set the glass next to him on the step. "What are you getting for school, Timmy?"

Cody asked, "Are you going to school here with us?"

When Timmy looked over at me, his eyes puzzled and worried,

I said loudly to the boys, "We haven't decided yet." I clipped the last clothespin on the line and walked over to the stoop. Picking up their empty glasses, I said, "Go finish your game now."

Timmy seemed relieved to have the conversation ended without having to explain to Jason and Cody that his school plans—in fact, his living plans—were still up in the air. As I carried the glasses into the kitchen and rinsed them in the sink, I thought how rootless he must be feeling. Not a good spot for a kid to be in.

A few days later, Jason and Cody invited Timmy along to Fredericksville when they went shopping for school supplies with their grandmother and their mother. I sent some money along with Bernice. "Let him pick out a few jeans and shirts," I said. "He's outgrowing the ones he brought with him."

"It's the fresh mountain air. Makes kids grow like weeds." Bernice stuffed the bills into her purse. The boys climbed into the backseat of her car, eager to be going, but Bernice turned to me and said out of their earshot, "Any more trouble with Garret?"

"Not a word. I haven't seen any sign of him. I checked the tent yesterday, and I don't think he's been back since we were there."

"Good. Let's hope he stays away."

I watched them drive off, Bernice in the driver's seat and the boys lined up in the backseat. They would pick up Bernice's daughter in Clayton on the way to Fredericksville.

While they were gone, I retreated to the loft and worked on the painting of Kate in the wicker chair. I was eager to finish it and move on to the next painting in the series, which I hoped Kate would pose for, too. I'd grown used to seeing her regularly and didn't want to give up our frequent contact.

Bernice tooted when they returned, and Timmy jumped out first. "Look at what I bought." He held up a new blue backpack. "It's full of pencils and stuff."

"That's neat," I said. "Did you thank Bernice?"

Stepping out of the driver's seat, Bernice said, "It was a successful trip, I think." She must have bought some new clothes for herself, too. She was wearing new light blue capris that clung to her ass and thighs. A scoop-neck matching top revealed a glimpse of bra straps.

"Seems to have been," I said. "Okay, Timmy, let's see your new clothes."

Timmy stepped back so I could look at what he was wearing: Wrangler jeans, a navy blue shirt that said *MAINE* across it in white letters, and Adidas sneakers. Jason and Cody filed out of the van, also wearing new duds.

"I said they could wear them home from the store for you to see, but they have to put old clothes on to play in." Bernice handed over a Wal-Mart bag with the clothes Timmy had worn earlier in the day.

"Quite a fashion show," I said. The boys seemed self-conscious. Timmy rubbed at the letters on his shirt, and Cody and Jason stuffed their hands into the back pockets of their stiff jeans.

"Give them a week or two. These new clothes will look as worn as the old ones," Bernice said.

Timmy butted in. "Aunt Sam," he said, "Bernice drove into the parking lot of the school in Clayton."

Bernice nodded. "Jason and Cody wanted to show him where they go to school."

Timmy went on, talking rapidly. "It's a little school, but Jason and Cody said it's pretty neat and the teachers are real nice. If I went there, I'd be in third grade, Cody in fourth grade, and Jason in sixth. We'd see each other all the time and have lunch and recess together every day."

"Is that what you want—to stay here and go to school?" I could see him pondering the question, probably thinking of his old friends back in Providence and his old familiar school.

Timmy hesitated, twirling a new red pencil between his thumb and finger. Finally, he said, "I guess it would be cool to go to school with Jason and Cody."

"Stay here, Timmy," both boys chanted.

"We'll give it some thought," I said. "We aren't going to decide right now."

Chapter 16

The elementary school was a squat brick structure that had three rooms: two classrooms and one all-purpose room. There were only nineteen students in the whole school, less than in Timmy's class alone in Providence. The principal took Timmy and me on a tour of the building. Mrs. Kramer, a pleasant woman with a gentle voice, was obviously proud of the school. She led us to the classroom that held kindergarten through third grades, where the desks were neatly lined in rows and the walls covered with colorful posters: a chart of the parts of speech, a map of the United States, and pictures of endangered species such as the African great frog.

"This is where you'll be, Timmy, if you join us," she said. "I'll be your teacher. We have thirteen students in this room, and five of them are in third grade. Mr. Harrington has grades four to six in the other classroom. You'll go to that room for language arts and reading."

We walked into the other classroom, and I heard Timmy reassure himself, "This is where Cody will be. And Jason, too."

Our last stop was the all-purpose room. "In here, we have art and music classes. We also eat here, everyone together, but usually with each room at its own table." When she said this, I could see Timmy picturing Cody and Jason at the next table.

"Where do you hold physical education classes?" I asked.

"When the weather permits, we go outdoors. Otherwise, we walk down the hill to the Town Hall for PE, even in the dead of winter."

Timmy's eyes grew big at this last comment. As we headed back to the kindergarten-to-third grade classroom, he seemed contemplative. I imagined he was comparing the school to his much larger one in the city. Here there would be only a handful of students in each class, and he would have to share a classroom with younger grades. The kid sitting in the next desk would be a stranger, not his old friend Darnell Watson who always sat next to him or across from him.

Mrs. Kramer pointed to bookshelves along the wall. "What do you like to read, Timmy?" Timmy shrugged his shoulders. So she picked out a book of jokes and a Matt Christopher baseball story and handed them to Timmy. "You can take these out on loan. They'll be due back when school starts."

Shyly, he took the books from Mrs. Kramer's outstretched hand.

"What do you say?" I prodded him.

"Thank you," Timmy mumbled as he slipped the books under his arm.

After we inspected the playground with its slide and jungle gym and basketball hoops, we said our goodbyes to Mrs. Kramer and left. On the ride back up the mountain, I tried to feel out Timmy's reaction to the school. "It's okay," he said, but he wouldn't offer any more. He changed the subject by reading from the joke book. "What's black and white and red all over?" he asked, keeping his place in the book with his index finger.

I smiled. This must be the oldest joke around. "A newspaper."

"Nope. An embarrassed zebra." But he didn't laugh at the joke, and he read silently to himself the rest of the way home.

Timmy continued to keep his head buried in the joke book as I fixed us a quick supper. While we sat at the table, he didn't comment on our visit to Clayton Elementary School, but he rattled on and on about Darnell Watson and his other friends in Providence. "Me and Darnell sit together at lunch," he said. "And then we go to recess, and us and our friends play kickball." And he talked about his mom and dad. "My mom let me have a sleepover with Darnell sometimes on Saturday nights. We'd eat pizza and play PlayStation. We stayed up really late, like midnight, and we slept in sleeping bags on the floor. My mom made waffles for breakfast, with bacon," he added, emphasizing the word *bacon*. "Then my dad took us to the Y, and we went swimming in the pool while he worked out."

All of this was during dinner, then he grew quiet again. We moved into the living room, and I handed Timmy the baseball book while I worked on a crossword puzzle. We sat together on the futon couch, Timmy at one end and me at the other. Once more, he got caught up in reading, his knees pulled up in front of him, his bare feet on the couch, his head bent toward the page. I was absorbed by crossword puzzles, and when I looked up later, he'd lain down and fallen asleep, his head at an awkward angle. *He can't be very comfortable. He'll wake with a crick in his neck.*

I reached over and pulled his head onto my lap. His hair was so fine and so blond, lying in wisps in the back of his neck. I stroked his forehead. He moaned a little and shifted his body, his feet dangling over the edge. I pulled his feet onto the couch, and he snuggled into me. *He must miss his mother's touch.* I was sure he missed everything about her—touch, smell, laugh. Especially the breakfasts she cooked, with bacon no less. I'd been a damn poor replacement, that was for sure. Stroking his forehead, I noticed how his eyelids twitched, the pale bluish flap covering his dreams. I wondered what he might be dreaming about—his mom, his dad, his house in Providence, his friends. I decided that I'd let him call Darnell in the morning; it might be good for him to hear a familiar voice.

When Timmy made the phone call in the morning, it didn't go as I'd hoped. At first, his voice was excited and eager, but as the conversation went on, it dropped into flat monosyllables. After he hung up, I said, "Was Darnell glad to hear from you?"

"I guess so."

"Well, what's he been doing all summer?"

"I dunno."

"Sure you do. You just talked to him. Has he been going to day camp?"

"Yeah."

"And?"

The words came out in a rush. "He's got a new friend. I don't think he even remembers that I'm supposed to be his best friend. All he talked about was this new kid he met at day camp, Jarmar Johnson. He said he slept over at Jarmar's house three times this summer, and Jarmar stayed at his house twice. That's more sleepovers than we ever had."

"Well, maybe Darnell and Jarmar are friends just because you aren't there right now. I'm sure Darnell still likes you."

"I don't think so. I think he's forgotten all about me. Him and Jarmar played baseball on the rec team. Darnell said Jarmar's a good player, and he can hit the ball pretty good. That's all he talked about: Jarmar, Jarmar, Jarmar. And he didn't even listen when I tried to tell him about getting lost in the woods and the bear and all that stuff."

I didn't know what to say. Of course Timmy was disappointed. This was another loss for him, another kind of grief. He moped in his room for the rest of the morning and just picked at his lunch.

I tried working in my studio, but I kept worrying about Timmy. I hated seeing him so downhearted again after things had been going so much better these last few weeks. I called Kate for advice. "Bring him down to the cottage this evening," she said. "There's a moose that feeds in the bay across the lake. We'll take a canoe ride over to see it. I think Timmy would get a kick out of that."

I jumped at the chance, though Timmy didn't seem excited about it.

We arrived shortly after supper to venture out to see the moose feeding at dusk.

The green Old Town canoe sat half in the water, half on the sand. A 2.5-horse motor was mounted on the side at the stern, and life preservers were stowed under the seats. Kate slipped an orange life preserver on Timmy and helped him buckle it. "Timmy, did you know that the moose is the state animal of Maine?" He shook his head and wouldn't look at her, so she took his hand and helped him climb into the middle seat. "I always find it fascinating to see a moose."

Still no response from Timmy. He sat quietly on the seat, gripping the gunwales.

Kate and I moved the canoe into the water a little way, then I sat in the bow. She pushed us off and, in one deft movement, climbed into the stern. For a while, we paddled with a nice rhythm. It felt good to be gliding across the water, and I hoped the adventure would lift Timmy's spirits, though at the moment he was being quiet.

As we ventured farther out, the bottom of the lake disappeared. Before long, it was black under us—black and deep and mysterious.

After a half hour, I pulled my paddle out of the water and lay it across the gunwales of the canoe. I called over my shoulder to Kate, "Are you getting tired? I'm running out of steam." The bay across the lake was still a good distance away.

Kate drew her paddle out of the water. "Let's get some power behind us." Lowering the small motor, she pulled on the rope until it coughed and started. We putt-putted along, and it took us a while to get across the lake.

As we neared the cove, I turned in my seat and called back to Kate, "Think we'll see the moose?" In the middle seat, Timmy sat hunched over, staring at the slatted floor of the canoe instead of looking at the scenery around him.

Kate called back, "We're getting close." Soon marsh grass began to brush against the bottom of the canoe and she cut the motor. We resumed paddling, moving almost silently among the lily pads in the bay. The only sound was the dip of our paddles. Suddenly, I heard Kate whisper, "Timmy, look over there. Near the edge of the shore."

Sure enough, an old cow moose was standing knee-deep in the bay, feeding on underwater vegetation. Her coat was dark, almost black, and she had high, humped shoulders. Her legs were skinny and gangly, the front ones longer than the back. She had a long, camel-like nose and ears like a mule.

Timmy's attention was caught by the ungainly animal. "She's funny looking. And big," he whispered. I could hear excitement in his voice. "I bet she's big as a horse!"

"She probably weighs around seven hundred pounds, I'd guess," Kate said. "Bull moose get a lot bigger than that. And they have huge antlers."

The moose looked over at us with a wary eye.

"She won't hurt us, will she?" There was worry in Timmy's voice.

"If she had a calf with her, she'd be nervous, and if she thought the calf was threatened, she might charge us," Kate said. "But this one seems pretty gentle. If we stay quiet and keep our distance, we'll be fine."

We watched the moose duck its huge head in and out of the lake to feed on water plants. As she chewed, water dripped from her lips and the flap of skin under her neck wobbled. "What's that under her chin?" Timmy asked.

"That's called the bell," Kate said.

"Why?"

"I guess because it's sort of bell shaped."

"Looks like a beard."

We watched the old cow longer than we should. The sun was beginning to go down, the sky tinted pink. "We'd better get back before it gets dark," Kate said. I nodded reluctantly and tore my gaze from the moose. We paddled until we were free of the lily pads and marsh grass, then she yanked the motor into gear.

I hadn't realized how quickly night fell on the lake. As we headed out toward the deeper water, the sun sank lower and lower. I felt a little spooked when the sky became as black as the fathomless water under us. We were swallowed by darkness. Kate switched on the green stern light, and we putted slowly, the canoe leaving a thin wake behind us. I zipped up my jacket and stuck my hands in the pockets.

The first sign of trouble was the sputtering of the motor. Then it died completely, and I heard Kate mutter, "Shit!" I swiveled in my seat to see what was wrong. She was kneeling in the canoe, yanking on the rope. The motor wouldn't catch. After several more fruitless tugs on the rope, she sighed heavily. "We're going to have to paddle the rest of the way."

"What's wrong, Aunt Sam?" Timmy asked, worry creeping

into his voice.

"We'll be fine, don't you worry," I said to reassure him.

"Hey, Timmy," Kate said, "see that yellow light way off in the distance?"

"Which one?"

By squinting my eyes and studying the horizon, I could make out dots of light, cottages along the distant shore. I had no idea which light Kate meant.

"Keep looking," Kate said. "Straight ahead."

Finally, I found it, a faint yellow light, and pointed it out to Timmy.

"I see it!" he said.

"That's the outside light at my cottage."

I couldn't believe how tiny and far away it looked, but I didn't want Timmy to know that I was beginning to have doubts that we'd ever see that cottage again.

"We have to get to that," Kate said, as she dug her paddle into the water.

The canoe bottom under my bare feet was cold, as if the icy depths of the lake were sending a warning through the wooden hull. A small chop had picked up on the surface. I had a moment of panic but didn't give in to it. Taking Kate's cue, I slipped my paddle into the water and tried to keep up with the pace she set.

I prided myself on being strong from cutting wood for the cabin stove, digging in the vegetable garden, mowing the uneven lawn, shoveling out in winter. But the going was rough, the huge lake resistant. We were headed directly into the waves, and they wanted to push us back. It seemed to me that we were making little progress. Whenever I didn't believe I could push the paddle one more time, I thought about Timmy and about getting him safely to shore.

Just when I was about to ask Kate if we could take a break from paddling, Kate began to sing behind me. "I am woman," she belted out. "Hear me roar!"

I wasn't sure I could remember all the words to Helen Reddy's classic, but Kate's determination came through in her voice, so I joined in. When I didn't think I could pull on the paddle one more time, I thought to myself, *Dig in, woman.* My shoulders ached, my arms felt ready to drop from the sockets, but I pushed on. Ever so slowly, the yellow light on the horizon grew larger.

When we finally got to shore, Kate and I beached the canoe. Timmy climbed out quickly, and I helped him out of his life jacket. I put my arm around his shoulder as we stood on the sand, looking out over the wide expanse of the lake that we had covered in the dark.

Exhausted, we staggered into the cottage, Kate holding Timmy's hand. She led him to the couch, where he curled into a ball and dozed off. I collapsed into a La-Z-Boy, and Kate shoved a can of Canada Dry ginger ale in my hand. I took a long thirsty drink. My arms trembled from the physical effort they'd made. I set the soda can on the floor and flipped the recliner back so that it was nearly horizontal. I closed my eyes, feeling utterly worn out.

I had nearly drifted off to sleep when I felt fingers on my shoulders, rubbing gently through my jacket. I smelled Kate, her delicious earthy scent. Kate was kneeling behind me, massaging my shoulders, neck, upper arms. At her touch, I felt the tension and tiredness begin to drain away.

At some point, Kate led me into her bedroom. She helped me take off my jeans, which were wet on the bottom cuffs, and I collapsed onto one of the twin beds that were separated by a small table with a lamp on it. "Thanks," I managed to mumble, as she tucked the comforter under my chin.

She leaned over me and lightly touched my cheek. "Didn't mean to wear you out," she said, cupping my face with her hands before she moved away from me. I loved the music of her voice, the light touch of her hand. I wanted more, but my eyes kept blinking shut from fatigue. I heard Kate getting ready for bed, pulling down the covers, fluffing up her pillow. And then undressing: slipping off her cotton slacks, pulling her sweatshirt over her head, unhooking her bra. I opened my eyes to see her standing next to her bed in only a pair of bikini panties, then she slipped her arms into a cotton pajama top and buttoned it. As she flipped off the light switch on the lamp, she said softly, "Good night." In the sudden dark, I heard the rustle of sheets as she crawled into her bed.

My eyelids fluttered heavily. I wanted to tell Kate how I hadn't thought I was going to be able to make it out there on the lake and how she kept me going. And how glad I was to see her warm and inviting cabin as we paddled in to shore. But sleep overtook me, and the words never made it past my lips.

I slept like the dead for several hours. Moonlight coming in through the window woke me, and for a few minutes, I felt disoriented. Then the soft purr of Kate's breathing reminded me that she was just a few feet away. I crept over into her bed and snuggled in next to her, wrapping my arms around her. She stirred in her sleep as I blew into her ear. Her eyes fluttered open, and she smiled. Slipping her hand behind my head, she pulled me toward her, her mouth ready with kisses. I began to fondle her, touching places I'd been aching to touch. Hurriedly, I unbuttoned her pajama top, and she gasped when my mouth found her breast. When she slid her fingers down my belly and under the band of my panties, I opened my thighs for her. We were both breathing heavily, trying to be quiet so as not to wake Timmy in the next room.

When I woke in the morning, I was still in Kate's narrow bed, but she was gone. I lay there for a few moments, smelling her scent in the sheets, relishing the memory of our first time together. When I finally roused from the bed, I saw that my jeans had been laid over a chair to dry. I pulled them on and tied my Reeboks. In the kitchen, I found a note on the table: "Good morning. I had to drive into Fredericksville for a meeting at the university. You and Timmy help yourself to whatever you can find for breakfast."

The coffee in the electric pot was still warm. While Timmy was sleeping on the couch, I poured a cup and carried it down to the shore. Leaning on the canoe and looking out over the lake, I tried to remember every moment of the previous night.

When Timmy woke, I drove him into Frederickson. We stopped at McDonald's for pancakes, then went to Wal-Mart where we bought a twenty-five-inch TV, a DVD/VCR combo, and a PlayStation. We also picked up a 'Jungle Book' video and a

'Backyard Baseball' game. I nearly gasped when the charges rang up on my credit card, but before we left town, I made arrangements to have a satellite dish installed at the cabin.

Timmy was thrilled with our purchases and helped me set up the TV in the living room when we got home. We wouldn't be able to get reception until the dish was installed, but he could watch videos and play games. For most of the day, he entertained himself with his PlayStation, so I was able to paint in my studio.

However, I couldn't keep my mind on my work; it kept drifting toward thoughts of Kate—her delicious smell, her lean body. We talked on the phone several times that day, fevered conversations, our voices filled with longing.

After Timmy went to bed and darkness rolled in, I went outside and sat on the steps. There didn't seem to be any stars. The sky was cloud-covered, and without starlight, everything seemed draped with black silk. In the dark, I couldn't see the mountains, but I felt their presence. I leaned my head back against the screen door, my mind racing with thoughts of Kate. I pictured her in her cottage by the lake. Maybe she was at the small table she used for a desk, typing away on her article. Or maybe she was sitting on the dock, looking out over the dark water, remembering the previous evening when we had paddled over to see the moose. And later, making love in her moonlit room. Perhaps she was asleep in the bed where I'd held her. Perhaps she was dreaming of me.

I decided to throw an end-of-the-summer party. On the front lawn, I set up two sawhorses and placed a wide board over them to make a serving table, then covered it with a red-checkered cloth. I sent Timmy to the flower garden to pick asters and marigolds for a centerpiece. I placed folding lawn chairs around a fire pit that I'd dug and ringed with stones, while Timmy carried logs from the stack by the woodshed and dropped them next to the fire pit.

That evening, the women gathered at my cabin for a potluck supper. I'd made a salad of red potatoes from my garden mixed with scallions, red and yellow peppers, fresh peas, and mayonnaise. And I sliced fresh tomatoes and cucumbers and dripped balsamic vinegar and olive oil over them.

I'd invited Bernice, but she declined, saying she had a meeting to go to. She didn't talk about being a member of AA, but I sure noticed that she seemed less belligerent than when I first moved here. I was beginning to like having her as a neighbor.

Kate was the first to arrive, carrying a bottle of Chianti in each hand. "*Buona sera*," she said, winking at me, and she leaned in to kiss me on both cheeks. She seemed happy; her face was glowing as she set the wine bottles on the table.

Jean's face was glowing, too, when she showed up with the blond, punk-haired woman I recognized as Ranger Hillby, though she was wearing black capris and a pink blouse instead of a brown uniform. "Hi, everyone," Jean hailed us. "This is Amy."

I introduced Amy to Kate, then offered them seats in the circle. Jean, meanwhile, was mobbed by Timmy claiming the huge bag of barbeque potato chips in her hand. He found a place to sit under one end of the picnic table, and soon his hands and mouth were stained orange as he devoured the chips. Badger stood at the end of the table, his tail wagging, waiting for any crumbs that fell his way. Jean handed Timmy a can of Mountain Dew, and I kept my mouth shut even as the soda disappeared in a few gulps.

I poured wine into clear plastic cups for the grown-ups. We were sitting around the fire pit, but we hadn't lit a fire yet. Kate glanced over at me then, and I felt a heat between my legs and a tingle that spread though my body. Unsettled, I said almost too gaily, "Well, let's bring on the snacks." I jumped up to get a plate of bruschetta from the table and passed it around the circle along with small paper plates and napkins. As we ate the bread and sipped wine, we settled into small talk, enjoying one another's company.

It didn't take long for Jean to begin telling jokes. "This man came into the store today and wandered up and down the aisles. It didn't seem he was finding what he wanted, so I asked if I could help him. He said he was looking for a box of tampons for his wife. I pointed him toward the right aisle, and a few minutes later, he set down a huge bag of cotton balls and a ball of string on the counter. I said, 'Sir, I thought you were looking for some tampons for your wife.' He replied, 'Well, yesterday, I sent my wife to the store to get me a carton of cigarettes, and she came back with a tin of tobacco and some rolling papers, saying it's a lot cheaper. So I figure if I have to roll my own, so does she.'"

Amy laughed the hardest of us all, seeming to really enjoy Jean's sense of humor. I looked back to see if Timmy was listening, but he'd left the crumpled, empty bag of chips on the table and was tossing a tennis ball for Badger to fetch. Badger was barking and nearly somersaulting as he leapt for the ball flying through the air, then carrying it back to Timmy. I watched them playing with the mangled tennis ball, Timmy not caring that it was slimy with Badger's drool.

Kate watched, too, then she looked at us and said, "By the way, what about those Red Sox?"

"Yeah," Jean said, "go Sox! This is their year, I just know it."

That set off a lively discussion of the Red Sox versus their archrivals, the Yankees. All of us were die-hard Sox fans, as were most New Englanders.

Just then, Jean called out to Timmy, "Hey, go look in the front seat of my truck. You might find something there."

He sprinted over to the truck. I heard the door open and close, and Timmy saying, "Wow." Then he came over to our circle, wearing a new baseball glove and holding up a ball still in its clear plastic wrapping. "This is cool," he said to Jean.

"It's yours."

"Really?"

"Yep," she said, getting up from the lawn chair. "And I'm going to give you a few pointers." She and Amy played catch with Timmy, tossing the baseball back and forth. Jean called out instructions: "Reach for it. Don't take your eyes off the ball. Cover the ball with your other hand when it gets to the glove."

Kate moved closer to me, and the skin of our arms rubbed as she refilled my wine glass. "Timmy's such a good boy."

"He is, isn't he?" I was surprised at the feeling of pride that welled up in my heart.

When it came time to eat, Jean lit the charcoal in her Weber grill, which she'd carried over in the bed of her truck. With a flair befitting Emeril, she cooked T-bone steaks for everyone but me. We moved our lawn chairs to the makeshift table, and Kate and I sat on one side with Timmy between us, Jean and Amy sat on the other side, and Badger lay under the table where he could count on getting some tidbits and steak bones. I filled my plate with a huge grilled portabella mushroom, potato salad, and vegetables.

"Let's make a toast," I said. We all raised our wine glass, and Timmy held a Mountain Dew can in the air. "To friendship."

"And more." Jean added, looking into Amy's eyes.

"To much more," Kate whispered, looking directly at me.

After the meal, we returned the lawn chairs to the circle around the fire pit. I tented a few logs with smaller twigs and balled paper, lit a fire, and added logs. When Jean brought out her guitar, we all started singing John Denver songs. With Badger lying beside him, Timmy rested against Kate's knee, waiting for the fire to burn down some so he could roast marshmallows. Kate showed him how to put a marshmallow on the end of a stick that Jean had whittled for him. Timmy leaned toward the fire, his face turned slightly to avoid the heat, and held the stick over a red ember, carefully allowing the white confectionery to puff up golden before it singed like charcoal. Then he pulled off the gooey mess, licking his fingers, and Kate helped him press it and a piece of Hershey bar between graham crackers. As he bit into the s'more, the smell of the campfire rose up around him, and shadows from the flames danced across his face. At that moment, he seemed more surrounded by family than he had since his parents died.

I'd been feeling very guilty about not visiting my mother. It had been months now since Dan died, and I knew I should drive down to Providence and give her some support. I dreaded it, though. Her stark grief terrified me; I wasn't sure I knew how to help her. Timmy, of course, was eager to see his grandmother, so we drove down on a Tuesday in August. This time, Kate was with us, and that made me feel better; it eased the burden somehow, just having her there beside me.

My mother looked awful, she'd lost weight, and her face was gaunt. She'd developed a habit of chewing her nails, and her fingertips were gnawed. Kate acted as though she and Mom were old friends from the minute we walked into the door of my mother's house. "Mrs. Warren, hello. I'm Kate, a friend of Sam's." She warmly grasped my mother's thin hand, ignoring the bleeding hangnail.

My mother seemed at a loss as to how to act; I could see her struggling to be graceful. "Glad to meet you," she murmured.

When she greeted me, my mother fell into my hug, and I felt tears on my neck. Her body was shaking with the attempt to control her sadness. "I'm glad you're here, Samantha," she said as she stepped back and reached for a tissue in her pocket to wipe her eyes. She took a moment to compose herself, then turned to Timmy, who still hung shyly near the door. "And Timmy, dear, look at you," she said. "You've grown at least two inches." That seemed to give him permission, so he ran to her and grabbed her at the waist, practically wrapping himself around her. My mother patted his head, and I saw a faint glimmer of a smile come onto her face.

That night, Timmy slept in the room that had once been his dad's, comforted by a familiar setting. He fell asleep hugging Pongo, his old stuffed Dalmatian.

My mother wanted to give Kate and me her bed, but we insisted she not give it up for us. She looked like she needed a good night's rest more than we did. So Kate slept on the living room sofa on top of a folded bed sheet, and I curled up on a sleeping bag on the floor next to her. It was too hot for covers. Through the window screen, we could hear the sounds of the city: sirens, cars, buses. "How do you think my mother is doing?" I whispered.

"Like she's been through a tragedy."

"I'm afraid she'll never get beyond losing Dan."

"Give her time," Kate said. "The wound is still recent. It'll probably never go away, but she'll learn to live with it."

"You always know how to make me feel better." I reached up for hand and tugged.

Kate slid off the couch and joined me on the sleeping bag. "Do you think they're asleep, your mother and Timmy?"

"Yes. Sound asleep." I kissed her neck. "They won't hear a

thing."

She snuggled into me, and we didn't need any more words between us. We relied on the language of love: kissing, fondling, rubbing our bodies together to ignite the fire we felt for each other.

The next day, Timmy was eager to go outside and connect with his old friends. He wasn't gone long.

"Wasn't Darnell home?" I asked.

"He was at Jarmar's house. I shoulda known that's where he'd be."

"What about Justin?" my mother asked. "Was he home?"

"Nah. He's at the summer rec program."

"Well, how about Matt?"

"He's coming over after he eats breakfast," Timmy said. "Is it okay if we play here, Grandma?"

"Of course, dear. He can even stay for lunch if he wants. I'll make grilled cheese for you."

Later when Kate and I left for downtown, Timmy and Matt were playing some game on PlayStation, and my mother was sitting in her recliner watching them while she drank her coffee. She seemed more peaceful than she had when we'd arrive the night before, and I realized how important it was to have her see Timmy as often as possible. I would need to make more visits in the future.

Kate and I went to the lawyer who had handled Dan's estate, and I talked to him about becoming Timmy's temporary legal guardian. Then we visited Timmy's school and picked up a copy of his records.

That night, we treated my mother to dinner at Angelo's, where Kate and I had the grilled vegetable lasagna, my mother ordered veal cutlet parmesan, and Timmy had the children's meat ravioli. Over the next few days, we packed up Timmy's favorite toys to take back with us, paged through photo albums, and shared stories about Dan. Timmy played with Matt, Justin, and Darnell occasionally, but he began to ask when he would see Cody and Jason again. On our last afternoon, my mother and Timmy went to the park, and I took Kate over to my old campus where we spent several hours at the RISD Museum.

My mother cried a little when we left for Maine early the next morning, but she seemed less distraught. It was evident that her grief had been lessened by our visit.

Chapter 17

Garret had been suspiciously absent from our lives. I didn't trust him and was on edge all the time, expecting him to show up or to do something malicious. The first indication I had that he was around again was a phone call from Jean. She was at the store. "Guess who just came in and bought a map of the mountains and a whole bunch of canned goods?"

"Garret?"

"You're right."

That afternoon, I was in the loft painting, and Timmy was on the other side of the studio at a small easel I'd set up for him playing with poster paints. At first, the knocking on the door didn't register with me. But then it grew into an insistent rapping, and I could hear someone shouting my name.

I set my paintbrush down and peered out the window. Looking down on the front step, I could see the top of a camouflage cap. Garret? When Jean had called to say he was in the area, I didn't expect him to show up at my front door. Nervously, I pondered whether I should answer the door. But then Timmy joined me at the window. "Aren't you going to see who it is?" he asked.

I decided that it would be okay to see what Garret wanted. I wouldn't let him in—I'd meet him on the front step. Timmy followed me downstairs, but I sent him to his room as a precaution. "Wait there until I say it's okay to come out."

"Is something wrong, Aunt Sam?"

"I don't think so. But we won't take any chances. Go on now."

With Timmy safely ensconced in his room, I went to open the wooden door. Garret's hand was in midair, his knuckles flexed to strike again. When he spotted me on the other side of the screen door, he let his hand drop. Through the wire mesh, I could smell the yeasty stench of beer on his breath, and I thought his balance was uneven as he leaned his shoulder into the doorframe. The only lock for the screen door was a hook-and-eye latch. With a furtive movement, I flipped the hook into the eyebolt. "What do you want, Garret?"

"I've got to talk to you. There's something important I want to discuss."

"I don't have anything to discuss with you. I think you should leave."

"Look here, don't go brushing me off. Just open that damn door and let me in."

"I'm busy right now," I said, trying to keep the anxiety out of my voice.

"Are you going to open that door or not?"

"Not. I want you to leave. And if you don't, I'm going to call the county sheriff."

"I need to talk to you!" Garret put his shoulder into the door and pushed, forcing the screen out of its track and causing the hook to flip out of the lock. I jumped back as he stumbled into the kitchen, knocking against me.

"Jesus! What are you trying to do?" I yelled.

"I said we're going to talk, and that's what I meant." Regaining his balance, Garret supported himself by leaning onto the table with both hands, palms down. I could see now that he was very drunk. His eyes were red and bleary, his hair stringy and looking like it hadn't been washed for days. His army green shirt hung outside his camouflage pants, but I could see the leather knife case hanging from his belt. I didn't know whether to be angry at his brutish behavior or frightened for Timmy and me. I didn't know how far Garret would go. But if he was the one who'd been causing all the trouble—tearing down my signs, skinning the raccoon, camping on my land, shooting at me—I should be very wary. His behavior had been irrational, and if he was as drunk as he seemed, he most probably would be even more irrational.

"Okay, let's sit down and talk, if that's what you want." I

needed to calm him before he did something rash, so I pulled out a chair and sat down. Across from me, Garret yanked a chair away from the table, but he nearly fell to the floor when he attempted to sit. Steadying himself by holding onto the table's edge, he managed to finally sit down.

"What's this about, Garret?"

When he talked, he slurred his words. "Remember our conversation earlier this summer? About me buying your land? It's time we stopped pussyfooting around. I expect you to sell it to me, this cabin and all." He pounded the table and gave me a sinister look. "This isn't any place for a woman, especially one from the city. You don't know how dangerous it can get out here all alone."

"I've been fine, and I plan to stay right here. I'm not interested in selling."

His face grew even redder, the flush spreading over his nose and cheeks. "Look," he said, "I intend to buy, so that means you're going to sell, whether you want to or not. And I'm not paying a sky-high price, either. You give me a good deal!"

His belligerent attitude infuriated me, making me thrust my shoulders back as I stood up. "I'm not interested, I've never been interested, and I never will be interested! Discussion closed. You might as well leave right now."

Garret sprang to his feet, knocking the chair over. It clattered on the pine floor. "Going to play tough, huh? Well, I can get tough, too." His hand went to the knife case at his belt, like a cowboy ready to pull his six-gun, though he swayed and fumbled.

Fear had me now, tightening my gut, speeding up my heart. I prayed that Timmy would stay quietly out of sight. "Garret, there's no need for this. We don't need a showdown about this. Just leave and let that be the end of it." I pointed to the screen door hanging on its hinges and tried to keep my voice steady.

"I'm not going anywhere," he shouted, pulling the door shut, "until I say so. And I'm not going alone."

"What do you mean by that?"

"I mean, Miss Highfalutin, that you're coming with me. You'll find that I'm serious about getting this piece of land. Maybe I can convince you to let it go cheap."

He sprung at me then, but I managed to slip out of his grasp. I was breathing hard and my knee throbbed where I bumped it on the table leg. Shuffling sideways, I backed away from him.

Garret glared at me. "Cat and mouse, huh? I can play that game."

Just then I heard Timmy's door open. *No,* I prayed, *don't let Timmy come out here.* But he did. He came down the corridor, his eyes wide and baffled. "Aunt Sam?" he said in a squeaky voice.

"It's okay, Timmy. Go back to your room. I'm all right."

He'd started back when Garret lunged at him and scooped him up. He held him around the waist with one hand, Timmy's legs flailing.

"Aunt Sam, Aunt Sam!" he cried, his fists pounding uselessly at Garret.

"Hey, settle down. I'm not going to hurt you. As long as your aunt does what I tell her to, that is." Garret held on tightly to Timmy and sneered.

"Come on, Garret." I said. "Think about what you're doing here. He's just a little boy. Put him down."

"Okay, I'll put him down," Garret said, but his free hand went to the leather case at his thigh, and he unsnapped it. "I'll put him down, but then you're both coming with me." He lowered Timmy until his feet reached the floor, then he slipped the knife from its case and extended the blade. "We're taking a little walk, the three of us."

My hand was at my throat, trying to calm my panic. "I'll come with you, but let Timmy stay here. He's frightened. Let him just stay here."

"Oh, he's scared, is he? Poor baby. I was scared the whole damn time I was a kid. Scared my daddy was going to swat me with his belt or the back of his hand. Hell, one time he damn near knocked out a tooth. See here," he said, pointing to a chipped front tooth with the knife. "I don't give a holy damn if this boy's scared." He lowered the knife toward Timmy's back, the tip pricking the fabric of his T-shirt.

I gasped. "Please, Garret."

"Come on now, you just open that door easy like and lead us outside. We'll be right behind you. Won't we, Timmy?" He shoved Timmy's shoulder with his free hand.

I moved to the door, though my legs felt as if I were wading through water. "Okay. We'll do what you say. Everything you say." I couldn't let Timmy be hurt.

As I made my way down the steps and out to the lawn, I heard Timmy whimpering and sniffling behind me, heard Garret staggering along in his army boots. Otherwise, it was eerily quiet; even the birds didn't seem to be singing. Quickly, I scanned the neighborhood, hoping to see any sign of Jean or Bernice.

Garret caught me looking around, and he laughed. "There's nobody here but us. Aren't we lucky? Just a cozy threesome out for a nice little walk. Now head down the logging road. And remember, I've got Timmy with me." He held the knife up so I could see the blade, the afternoon sun glinting off steel.

Forcing one foot in front of the other, I struggled to keep my footing as we followed the logging road toward the back end of my property. We hiked downhill, and all the while I pictured the blue tent waiting for us.

"Unzip it," Garret instructed. "The tent, stupid. Unzip the flap."

I did what he asked, even though I knew that going into the tent was not a good idea. Timmy and I might not come back out alive.

Garret jabbed me in my back with his fist, shoving me through the opening. My bruised knee hurt as I landed on it, making me cry out. Timmy came hurtling in after me, and we ended up in a heap on the tent floor. Then the zipper zinged shut. Garret was pacing and muttering outside. I had no idea what he was up to.

I heard the metal trunk open, heard the rustling of papers, which I knew must be the map and blueprints Bernice and I had discovered. Then the lid slammed shut, and no more noises came through the tent fabric.

Timmy was huddled in a ball, whimpering, his eyes wide with fright. "Hey, come here," I said, pulling him closer to me. As we

165

sat on the tent floor, I held him in a tight embrace. "We'll be all right. You just wait and see. He's just a big bully—he's not going to hurt us."

Timmy hiccupped, wiped his nose on the back of his hand, and burrowed into my lap. "What's he mad about?"

"He wants something he can't have."

"Can't you give it to him—what he wants? Then he'll let us go."

Looking down at Timmy's tear-stained face, I wavered. There was a lot at stake here—Timmy's safety was paramount. But there was also my cabin and the spread of land on this mountain that I'd worked so hard to make my own. How did I ever weigh the two—Timmy's well-being and my own dreams? And what would I be teaching him if I yielded to Garret's demands? Finally, I said, "I can't do that, Timmy. It wouldn't be right to give in to him. You've got to trust me on this, okay?"

"I guess."

Holding him in the crook of my arm, I smoothed his damp, blond hair and realized I had to make my promise come true. Somehow I had to get us out of this mess.

Time seemed to move slowly while we waited to see what Garret had planned for us. He was stirring outside, mumbling to himself, then I heard a thudding crash as he must have tripped over something and fell to the ground. The tent buckled for a moment, then righted itself. He'd fallen right in front of the flap; the shadow of his body darkened the only way out. Timmy started, but I calmed him and motioned for him to be quiet. We waited for Garret to get to his feet. I expected cursing and feared he'd be angrier than ever and take it out on us. Instead, after a few minutes, we heard snoring. He'd fallen asleep—or into a drunken stupor.

On my knees, I crept toward the door and tried to tug at the zipper to open it. Garret was wedged against the flap. There was no way to open it without waking him. And if I got the zipper open, how would Timmy and I sneak past him?

It was best to settle back and consider the possibilities. The afternoon sun filtered through the tent fabric, heating the inside. It was stuffy and close in the tiny space, and I could see that, despite our perilous situation, Timmy was growing drowsy. His breathing slowed and came in regular breaths as he gave in and dozed, sprawled on the floor of the tent. His snoring was soft, feathering from his lips, an echo to Garret's loud, sputtering snores.

Looking down at Timmy's face, I thought, even in the middle of this turmoil, he feels safe enough to sleep when I'm near him. And then another thought came into my mind: If we get out of this alive, I'm not going to let this little boy go.

Timmy's head was nudged against my thigh. I shifted away from him gently so as not to wake him. On my hands and knees, I scrounged around the tent, searching for something I could use for our escape. Near a hand-held can opener, I found the top of a can, its edges jagged and sharp. With the tin lid in one hand, I shuffled toward the back of the tent and felt around the fabric with my other hand for a good place to begin cutting. I found a seam that had weakened and begun to separate. Using the can lid like a razor, I sawed at the seam where the side of the tent met the floor. The work was slow, the can cover not as sharp as I had hoped. I paused every so often to listen for Garret, then emboldened by his loud snoring, I resumed my task. I'd made a slit about two feet long that was parallel to the floor and had just begun to work upward from the center of the slit. I wanted an opening large enough for Timmy and me to sneak through, and I had to work fast to finish it before Garret woke.

I didn't know how much time passed as I worked, the slit gradually growing longer. Another foot, and I could wake Timmy. But Garret woke first. At the sound of movement, I looked to see his shadow struggling to move to his feet. It was as though he didn't remember where he was. "What the shit?" I heard him mumble.

Quickly, I plopped down on the floor and hid the can top under my leg. I kept my back to the slit and hoped Garret wouldn't notice it behind me. When I heard the zipper's teeth opening, I pulled Timmy's head onto my lap. He stirred but didn't wake. Garret stuck his head through the door flap and seemed surprised to see us. "What the fuck?" he said, shaking his head as if to clear it. He finished unzipping the flap and stumbled into the tent. His eyes were bleary and unfocused, and he seemed confused as he rubbed his face and scratched the stubble on his chin. A growing recognition seemed to come to his eyes, and he muttered, "Shit! What a mess."

"Garret," I said, "sit down here and get your bearings." I saw a chance to talk him out of holding us hostage. He sat down clumsily on top of his sleeping bag, crossing his legs. I noticed with relief that the knife was back in its sheath.

"Don't he look cute?" he sneered, looking at Timmy. "All cuddled up like that."

"Do you know his story, Garret? What Timmy's been through?"

He brushed aside my words. "Haven't we all been through something or other? Life isn't a bed of roses for anybody."

"His parents died, my brother and his wife," I said. "In a car accident. Just a few months ago."

This seemed to catch him by surprise, and he glanced down at Timmy. Then he scoffed, "That's not always so bad. I'd have been a hell of a lot better off if my folks had died when I was a kid."

His callousness shook me, and I nearly gave up, considering it hopeless to try to talk to him.

"Nobody ever gave me a lap to snuggle in," Garret mused. And then he began to talk, almost as if it were to himself. "It's about time for life to give me a break. I haven't ever had anything given to me. Talk about your school of hard knocks, I'm the number one graduate. There were seven of us kids and my ma and pa. Any money that come in went right back out at the liquor store."

Garret wiped sweat from under his neck with his hand, then wiped his hand on his pants, before he continued. He talked, but it wasn't really to me. It was more an oral remembering for him. "We bounced around a lot, but I do remember this one house we lived in. I suppose it might have been a decent house once, but by the time we moved in, it'd seen better days. Jesus, it was cold in the winter. We tore up the furniture and burned it to stay warm. The summers seemed easier. Us kids got along without shoes, and we hardly needed clothes except the secondhand bathing suits my ma picked up at the thrift shop. Our hair got so long, it got all tangled up with briars from playing out in the field. My sister Marianne had a gob of gum in her hair, I swear it was there from June to August. Even going swimming wouldn't budge it, it was stuck so tight. It wasn't until it was time for school to start and Ma got ready to shear the sheep that that gum came free. Do you know what that's like, getting your head sheared like a damn sheep? Ma made the seven of us line up, and she came at us. I tell you, the kids at school got a big laugh out of my shaved head."

Garret pulled off his camouflage cap and scratched over his ear, almost as if he was checking his own head of hair. "You know," he said as he placed the cap back on his head, "I think Marianne was kind of sad to see that gum go. It was like she'd grown used to it being there. She kept fingering the spot where it'd been, and it was real gentle the way she kept patting that bare spot. Yeah, gentle, like how she handled her doll. Hell, the most softness I ever saw in my family was Marianne crooning over her doll. And even that was knocked out of her by the time she had her own kid at sixteen."

I thought maybe his rambling indicated that he was sober enough now to be reasoned with. "Garret, you can see what a bad idea this is, can't you? If you do anything to hurt us, you'll be in big trouble. Let us go, and I won't press charges. You can take the tent down, forget about my land, and go on about your life."

"Ha! What life? My old lady is just a big headache, and yesterday I lost my job at the mill! If I don't get this land, I won't have nothing ahead of me."

"Why is my land so important to you? You don't really like fishing, it seems. Why do you want to live up here?"

"Hell, who said I was going to live here? That's as much as you know." He laughed. "There's other uses for this land, you know."

I thought of the blueprints Bernice and I had found. "Like what?"

"Like maybe there could be a nice ski slope here. A place where people would pay to come for skiing and snowboarding.

169

Your cabin could be expanded into a lodge. What's that fancy word? Chalet? It could be a ski chalet. Can't you just see the kiddies drinking hot cocoa and their folks sipping on hot toddies? Think of the money they'd be spending."

"Think of the money it would cost to build a ski slope here. You'd have to clear the land and build the trails. You'd need lifts and grooming equipment. Probably lights for night skiing. You're talking hundreds of thousands of dollars, Garret, and that's not even counting promoting it so people know about it. Where are you getting that kind of money?"

"Who says it's me putting up the dough?" His voice took on a bragging tone. "I'm working with some developers from out of state. Big shots with pockets bulging with cash."

I didn't know whether to believe him or not. Did he really have the financial backing of developers, or had he just let his imagination run wild? "Who's behind it?"

"Nobody you know. Some guys from Massachusetts. I met them at a wedding, my wife's niece. Free beer was flowing like water, and we were all pretty tanked. But we had a good conversation, and I remember it word for word. These guys got to talking about Maine as a vacation spot. One of the guys is a skier, and he said why aren't there more ski resorts in the state. Said there was money to be made if someone was to build a ski slope. Next thing you know, I cooked up this deal with them to find some available land. First thing that came to my mind was the Clayton area. It's plenty busy around here in the summer with all the vacationers from out of state, but in wintertime, it's damn near dead. I heard Bernice's son-in-law talking at the mill about the cabin she owned up here, so I decided to get friendly with her. I nosed around to find out if there was any mountain land for sale. Bernice spilled the beans about you buying this place not too long ago. Said she thought it was unusual for a city woman to settle here. And I thought, ah-ha, there's a soft touch. Maybe living on the land is a lot harder than what she's cut out for. Maybe she can be convinced to sell it cheap. So I hiked up here and, sure enough, your property's sitting right in the ideal spot. And if I get my hands on it, I'll make me a nice profit."

"Why my land? There's hardly room here for a ski slope."

"You don't know everything. The land next to you, all those acres the mill owns, is going up for sale. Then there'll be plenty of room for a decent-size ski slope. I figured it wouldn't take much to scare you into selling. You'd go high-tailing it back to where you came from. And I'd make some easy money."

"Easy," I said. I pointed at Timmy asleep in my lap. "You find it easy to terrify a little boy. To hold a knife to his back and threaten his life. What kind of a man are you?"

I'd made a mistake. This angered him, and he reached toward his knife. "I can scare the shit out of a woman, too," he said, staring at me. "Hell, I could slit your throats real easy. Bury you both in the dirt floor of that old cellar hole, cover you over with leaves, and by the time anyone found you, you'd be nothing but a pile of bones."

"Wait, Garret. Let's just take a deep breath here. You don't want things to get out of hand."

He unfastened the knife case and ran his thumb along the hilt. "Maybe I do. Maybe that's exactly what I want."

At that time, a hand reached through the narrow opening I'd made and patted my lower back. I knew at once that it was Jean. Her fingers pressed on my back briefly, then the hand withdrew and I heard her move stealthily around the tent. I understood that I was to keep Garret distracted. "Now think things over," I said to him. "You don't want to get into a bigger mess. Let Timmy and me go, and no one has to even know about this."

Just then, the tent door flap was pushed open by the barrel of a rifle. It was aimed at the back of Garret's head. Jean said, "Don't even think about getting that knife out, Garret. I've got a 30.06 pointed right at your skull. I've been deer hunting for twenty years, and I'm a damn good shot. Not that anybody would miss at this close range."

Timmy startled awake, and he started to jump up. Quickly, I pulled him down and covered his body with mine.

"Hey, hey, take it easy," Garret said, turning toward Jean and holding up his hands, palms outward. "Don't go ballistic on me."

"You're the one who's been ballistic, buddy. Now get to your feet and come out of that tent."

"All right, I'm coming. Just put that gun down." Sweat ran down Garret's brow.

"I'm not putting it down until you're behind bars," Jean said.

Garret swore under his breath, shrugged his shoulders in a gesture of defeat, and started to leave the tent.

"Just a minute. I'll take this on your way out," I said, pulling the knife out of the sheath at his belt.

As Garret crawled out of the tent, Jean stepped backward from the door flap, keeping the rifle pointed at him.

When the tent was empty except for the two of us, I scooped up Timmy and asked, "You okay?" Timmy wordlessly threw his arms around my neck and buried his face in my chest. "It's all over now," I said, rubbing his back. "Everything's going to be all right."

We went out of the tent into the sunlight. Jean was standing over Garret, who sat on a log by the dead fire, his shoulders hunched over.

Timmy seemed emboldened seeing Garret at the end of a rifle. He hung behind me, but he said to him, "Are you the man who skinned the raccoon and hung it in the tree?" I'd almost forgotten that incident, but it must have made a deep impression on Timmy.

Garret raised his eyebrows and mocked, "What if I am?"

"That was a bad thing to do," Timmy said.

Garret mimicked in a falsetto voice, "That was a bad thing to do. Boo-hoo."

"Okay, that's enough out of you," Jean said, kicking Garret's foot with her hiking boot.

Timmy tugged at my shirt, and I leaned over to hear him whisper, "It was a bad thing, wasn't it, Aunt Sam?"

I patted his shoulder and reassured him. "Yes, honey, it was. But he's not going to do any more bad things to us." Turning to Jean, I said, "You showed up just at the right moment. How did you know to come here?"

"It was damn good detective work, if I do say so. This bozo showed up at the store, drunk in the middle of a weekday," she said, pointing at Garret with the rifle, "which seemed odd to me. After he left, I got to thinking about all the supplies he bought. I put two and two together, and it made sense that he might be coming up to the mountain. That's when I phoned you to warn you. After we hung up, I called Bernice, and she told me Garret got canned at the mill. Then I was really worried about you. So I drove up here right away. When I checked your cabin, your Jeep was there, but you and Timmy weren't. And there were signs of a struggle: the front door was hanging open, and there was a chair tipped over in the kitchen. The next obvious choice was to check Garret's tent."

"I didn't think you even knew where the tent was."

"Oh, I've walked down here a few times, checking it out. I just hadn't told you about it."

"I'm damn grateful you're here today," I said. Jean nodded, then I asked, "Now what do we do?"

"Get him back to your cabin and call the county sheriff." She poked at Garret's shoulder with her finger. "Get up and get going, buster." When he didn't budge, she poked again, this time with the barrel of the gun. "I said to move it."

We must have made quite a parade walking up the hill. Garret led, with Jean and the rifle at his back. Pulling up the rear was Timmy and me, holding hands. I couldn't help but notice how clean the air smelled and how blue the sky was with its few cirrus clouds. How lovely it was here on the mountain.

Chapter 18

Kate and I would have a whole evening to ourselves. For the first time since Timmy had come here, we would be completely alone.

Jean and Amy had taken Timmy to the movies in Fredericksville. After the show, they were stopping for Moose Tracks ice cream cones at Gifford's. They wouldn't bring Timmy home before eleven that night. I was sure that Jean and Amy had schemed up the plan to let Kate and me have some time alone. They would have to be blind not to see the relationship that was growing between us.

I took a long bath, soaking in bubbles up to my neck. Then I rummaged through my closet for something sexy to wear. I found a pair of black linen slacks and a black camisole that I hadn't worn since my days as an art curator in Providence.

I was daubing perfume on my wrists when Kate knocked on the door. My stomach began to tighten—butterflies on the rampage—as I went to let her in. She stood on the step with the outside lamp shining down on her, highlighting her dark hair and compelling gray eyes. She wore tight-fitting stone-washed jeans and a white oxford shirt, the sleeves rolled to expose her lovely arms, and a brown leather vest. Freshly picked purple coneflowers were clutched in her fist, and she handed them to me as she stepped into the kitchen.

I put the flowers in a vase and set them on the coffee table in the living room. It was chillier than usual for the end of August, a prelude of the coming fall and winter months, so I lit a fire in the grate and closed the glass doors to hold the heat in. The fireplace cast warmth and light at us while we sat on the futon couch and toasted each other with chardonnay.

"To the absence of Garret from your life," Kate said, raising her glass.

I wanted to say *and to the presence of you in my life*, but instead I clinked her glass with mine and smiled. We nibbled on stuffed mushrooms and pita bread with hummus as we sipped the wine. Several times, we refilled our glasses as we talked.

After a pleasant interlude of chatting, I said, "I have a treat for you. Put this over your shoulders." I wrapped an afghan around her like a shawl, then slipped into a lavender cardigan myself. Lifting a covered wicker basket from the coffee table, I said, "Here, take this," and shoved the basket into her hands.

"What's in it?"

"Mussel shells. We'll need matches. There's some on the fireplace mantel. We can get them on our way out."

"Our way out? What are you planning?"

"You'll see. Then I grabbed the matches from the mantel and led Kate outside. "Follow me." We headed down the path toward the stream.

Walking beside me, she joked, "I don't know if I should trust you…"

"I haven't led you astray yet, have I?"

She laughed. "Oh, yes, deliciously so. And I hope you will again."

"The night is just beginning," I said, resting my head on her shoulder for a moment.

When we reached the stream, I knelt on the bank. "Pass me the basket, will you?"

"Your little bag of tricks?" she asked, passing it to me.

"Sort of." I reached in and took out a mussel shell that I'd made into a candle by filling it with wax and a wick. I struck a match on a rock, lit the wick, and slipped the shell gently into the water. It floated like a miniature sailboat, its mast a flickering flame.

Beside me, I felt Kate's breath in my ear. "How lovely. Let me do one," she said softly. She took a shell from the basket and lit the wick, then placed it on the water.

We kept lighting the little candles until we'd set them all afloat. They bobbed and drifted like little stars on the surface of the stream. We stood on the bank, our arms around each other, and watched until they winked out, one by one, leaving a warm red glow that lasted after the flame died.

I left the empty basket there, and we started back up the path toward the cabin, using the flashlight to show the way. We kept stopping to kiss, leaning into each other, pressing our bodies together. When we finally reached the lawn, I tugged the afghan from Kate's shoulders and spread it on the grass. Sinking down onto the afghan, I pulled at Kate's hand. She stretched out beside me, curling her arms under her head. I lay my head on her chest and listened to the steady rhythm of her heart, remembering the time we'd watched the stars together in this same spot. The night was chilly, but I didn't feel cold so close to Kate's body. When she said, "Come here," I moved up beside her and we necked like a couple of teenagers. We reached a point when we couldn't wait any longer, so we pulled each other up and stumbled into the cabin.

Out of sheer desire, in our rush to be together, we began stripping our clothes the moment we were inside the door. Kate wiggled out of her leather vest and peeled off her jeans, and I unzipped my slacks and stepped out of them. And at the same time, we were kissing and making our way across the room. In a mood of abandon, we left a trail of discarded shoes and socks and clothes. "Help me with this," I said, and we flipped the futon into a bed. Standing between the futon and the fireplace, I hurriedly unbuttoned her blouse. The fire snapped and glowed as the blouse drifted to the floor. Kate unclasped her bra and dropped it, revealing her lovely breasts, the nipples hard, a temptation for my mouth. I sat down on the futon and pulled her close, placing my lips on her breast. She ran her fingers through my hair and moaned. Then she knelt in front of me and freed my arms from the lavender sweater. We lay down, laughing as our elbows knocked together in our rush to remove each other's panties.

"You are so dear to me, Samantha," Kate said softly, and I noticed that her voice had turned thick. She rolled over on her side, facing me, and we reached for each other hungrily. I put my hands around her waist and pulled her to me. Slipping one hand under my camisole, she inched her fingers up to my breast. I trembled all over. She pulled the camisole over my head, and we began to kiss again, our fingers roaming each other's skin.

After we made love, we lay quietly on the futon, watching flames in the fireplace throw a choreography of light and shadows on the pine walls and high ceiling. I was intoxicated by her touch, her nearness. I thought if I died right at that moment, I would go to heaven happy: Kate's head buried in my shoulder, her hair smelling of musk perfume.

Right after Labor Day, Timmy became a student at the Clayton Elementary School, though I'd made no formal arrangement for him to stay with me permanently. It just seemed to fall into place that way. I'd registered him in the third grade. He seemed to settle in well. He liked Mrs. Kramer, made new friends with the four other kids in his grade, and enjoyed seeing Cody and Jason at lunchtime and recess. Bernice had retired from the mill, had sold her house, and was living full time at her cabin across the road, so Timmy got to play with them after school some days, too, when they were visiting their grandmother.

Timmy very seldom asked any more about returning to Providence, though he did miss his own grandmother. I promised that we would see her at Thanksgiving. My plan was to leave the mountain during deer hunting season. It was a compromise of sorts. I hadn't posted my land again, and I was just going to leave the matter up in the air. That meant—at least to Jean, I'm sure— that I would probably never hang the orange and black posters. Not making a decision was a way of making a decision, I suppose. At this point, I certainly couldn't refuse to let Bernice and her son-in-law hunt on my property, and how could I turn away the townsfolk, all hunters, who had helped search for Timmy the day he'd been lost on the mountain?

At the start of the new semester, Kate gave up the lake cottage she'd been renting and moved back to her apartment in Fredericksville. She'd finished her writing article and gone back to teaching her fall classes in women's history. She spent most weekends with me, and Timmy seemed to miss her almost as much as I did when she wasn't around.

An amazing thing happened that fall: the Red Sox beat their old nemesis the Yankees to win the American League Championship. They went on to face the Cardinals in the World Series. Jean and Amy were beside themselves with excitement; Timmy and I walked over to Jean's house to watch the first three games of the series with them.

For the final game against the Cardinals on October 27, we all gathered at my cabin with Kate joining us. Timmy sat close to the new TV, wearing an official Red Sox hat Kate had brought him. We all hooted at the Cardinals and hollered every time the Red Sox made a play, Timmy raising his fist in the air and calling out, "Way to go!" Each time he raised his arm, his father's watch—which he had taken to wearing once in a while—slid from his wrist halfway to his elbow. I smiled as I watched him push it back into place, his fingers lingering a moment on the silver links.

When Keith Foulke fielded the ball and threw the last batter out to seal the win, Kate jumped up from the futon, pulled me up with her, and yelled so loudly that Badger yelped. Timmy sprang up from the floor, shrieked, and hugged Kate and me. Jean and Amy were dancing, singing, "Oh, yeah, oh, yeah!" It was a celebration of winning against all odds. The Red Sox had won the World Series and broken an eighty-six-year jinx.

After the ball game, we sat around the living room and played charades. Timmy was acting out a word, pulling on his ear, and making frantic swirling motions with his hand. I got up to put another log on the fire, then turned to look at my friends gathered here. I knew if Timmy stayed with me, I would not be alone in raising him. Hillary Clinton had it right when she repeated the old African adage: It takes a village to raise a child. In this case, it was a village of women.

One Saturday, Timmy, Kate, and I walked along the old logging road. The earthy scent of autumn was heavy and sweet in the air. Milkweed pods were spilling their cottony package of seed, and the sumac was fiery in color.

As we walked, Timmy chatted about the project he was making for art class. He was collecting leaves for his project, and he stooped often to pick up yellow beech leaves or orange oak leaves. In a serious manner, he chose the best and dropped them into a plastic Ziploc bag that Kate was carrying.

With my hiking boots, I kicked at a pile of bright red leaves that had dropped from a sugar maple. Seeing that splotch of red suddenly made me think of the red paint Timmy had squirted all over my painting earlier that summer. In the light of all that had happened, I could finally see the humor in that and I started laughing. I slipped my arm around Kate, and as we walked, I whispered to her, "I was thinking of the painting of you that Timmy smeared with red paint. Doesn't that seem like a long time ago?"

"Ages" she said, laughing.

"What's so funny?" Timmy asked, coming up to us with a yellow leaf in his hand. Kate held out the bag for him.

"Oh, nothing. And everything," I said. "I just feel happy all of a sudden." It came to me that at the beginning of the summer, Timmy had seldom laughed. Nowadays, he giggled when playing with Cody and Jason or when Kate teased and tickled him. I realized how I wanted to hear joy erupt from his mouth, from his heart.

I looked down at his blond head, at the narrow width of his shoulders. And I looked over at Kate and thought about what she had once said about how we don't see things that are right in front of us. Maybe it had been there all along—Timmy's fated journey to my house.

I knelt down so that I was closer to his height. I felt Kate's hand on my shoulder. "Timmy," I said, "I know I can never take the place of your mom and dad, but I want to give you a home. I'm going to look into adopting you so you can stay with me. Does that sound all right to you?"

He looked me in the eye, and I could see how desperately he wanted that—to have a home again, a family. In a small voice, he asked, "For a long time?"

"A very long time."

Timmy nodded solemnly but didn't make any move toward me. *It was up to me,* I realized. I would have to make all the right moves, show him it was okay to love again. That it was safe. Without hesitation, I stood and pulled him to us, to Kate and me. The three of us hugged, while all around us the fall colors raged brilliantly.

About the Author

Laurel Mills grew up near the low mountains of Maine and especially enjoyed the summers at Weld on the sandy beach of Webb Lake. She now lives in Wisconsin with her partner of twenty-seven years, and they spend summer days biking gravel trails that are bordered by cornfields and hayfields. In the winter, Laurel hunkers down and writes. She is working on *Taking Flight*, a novel about a birder and the abused woman she falls in love with.

Laurel is the author of the novel *Undercurrents* (Rising Tide Press) and of four award-winning books of poems, including *I Sing Back* (Black Hat Press). Her work has been published in *Ms. Magazine, Yankee, Calyx, Kalliope, Common Lives: Lesbian Lives*, and the anthology *Boomer Girls: Poems by Women from the Baby Boom Generation*. She is Senior Lecturer Emeritus at the University of Wisconsin-Fox Valley, where she taught English and edited the literary magazine *Fox Cry Review*. She is happy to be newly retired and devoting more time to writing and to teaching writing workshops.

She can be reached through her Web site www.laurelmills.net and welcomes correspondence from readers.

Intag titles

Printed in the United States
129387LV00004B/9/P

9 781933 113920